SOLDIER'S HEART

A Tale of Love and Conflict In Civil War Missouri

JEREMY WEBB RUSK

R*R*P

RUTLEDGE ROAD PRESS

Belmont, Massachusetts

Fictional characters are introduced or developed in this historical narrative to allow for the presentation and interpretation of overarching events and social and cultural attitudes. In all cases they are the product of the author's imagination. Any resemblance to actual events or locales or persons, living or dead, is entirely coincidental.

ISBN 978-1-4507-8132-9

Rutledge Road Press
5 Rutledge Road
Belmont, Massachusetts 02478
www.soldiersheartcivilwar.com

To My Grandfather
WILLIAM FANTLEY WEBB
Blacksmith, Carpenter, Musician
Son of This Story's Protagonist

He taught me about the many ways men
can do things with their minds and hands
and that in everything one does
the goal should be excellence.

INTRODUCTION

In the words of a scholarly wag, "history is a pack of tricks we play on the dead." While it is true that complete objectivity and accuracy in historical writing is impossible, such an assertion is skeptical in the extreme. *Soldier's Heart* has been conceived as a "non-fiction novel," a term coined by Truman Capote to describe his book *In Cold Blood*. It takes a more optimistic view of the nature of historical understanding and the writing of history. Not only is it possible as the Oxford philosopher, historian, and archaeologist, R. G. Collingwood, contended, to re-enact the past, there is a sense in which the historian can understand the past better than it understood itself. Looking back through time on men and their lives, the historian has the benefit of distance which allows him to see the larger context in which past events take place—both the full richness of what preceded an era and the complicated consequences that followed from it.

This non-fiction novel in certain respects takes that claim a step further. If a work is grounded in thorough research and has a lively narrative flow, it can capture the essence of a period in ways that often elude the pure historical study. One of the best examples of that view, as cited by Harvard Professor Robert Coles, is the nineteenth century work of Mary Anne Evans, who wrote the classic British novel, *Middlemarch*, under the male nom de plume "George Eliot." She thoroughly immersed herself in a wealth of historical sources, in the beliefs and prejudices of an era, the customs, even the dialects of the English provinces during the age that immediately preceded her. In Coles' view she produced a "novel of manners, a philosophical novel, a psychological novel," a Victorian novel in a class by itself. It captured a time and place in ways that surpassed the best traditional histories of the period.

Soldier's Heart is set in southwest Missouri in the last half of the nineteenth century, a time and place of great tumult and significance for the future of the young republic, but one inadequately covered by traditional histories of the period. The border area of Missouri and Kansas pulsated like atrial fibrillation in the heart of a nation sick with the disparity between the persistent institution of slavery and the republic's foundational declaration that all men are created equal. A number of key events and important legislative and judicial actions having to do with slavery in the rapidly expanding frontier were focused in that section of the country: the Missouri Compromise of 1820; the Kansas-Nebraska Act of 1854; the murderous attack of the abolitionist John Brown at Pottawatomi, Kansas (a prelude to his raid on Harper's Ferry); the Supreme Court decision in the Dred Scott case, 1857.

Bloody conflict escalated in Missouri and Kansas before the Civil War erupted and raged throughout the war which, arguably, actually began, as reported then by the New York Times, with the first pitched battle between Union and Confederate forces at Carthage, Missouri, on July 5, 1861. And the turmoil continued well after Lee surrendered at Appomattox as families of both factions, who had been caught up in murderous neighbor against neighbor conflict, returned to Missouri from exile in Kansas and Texas, hoping to rebuild their lives. Whereas the war in many areas of the country was primarily army against army, nowhere in the nation did the civilian population suffer more than in the Missouri-Kansas border area.

This tale follows the fate of two southwest Missouri families who, unaware of what the future held for them, sought new opportunities in the Missouri frontier just as pre-war hostilities began to erupt. Jonathan Rusk and Nancy Rusk came from Indiana in 1849 with their large family. A few years later in 1856 Elijah and Martha Jane Webb, along with their children and slaves, came west from Overton County, Tennessee. The experiences of these two clans provides unique insight into a time and place inadequately covered in the major histories of the Civil War. More than that, the patriarchs of these two families are my paternal and maternal ancestors.

To speak of writing a non-fiction novel is to describe a process that is in the first instance heavily grounded in fact ranging from general historical studies to local histories, descriptions of military equipment, accounts of battles and visits to battle sites. More specifically focused resources include family oral histories, land maps and property deeds, civil court cases, birth, marriage and divorce documents, census records, letters, family photos, obituary notices and on the ground searches for homestead sites and tombstones.

Beyond the kind of research that undergirds traditional histories there is in the non-fiction novel the challenge of creating a lively narrative and developing authentic characters. The Welsh poet, Gwyn Thomas, said, "All writers are liars. How else could we hope to caress the truth?" In what I like to think of as "truthful lies" I have imaginatively and with caressing care dared to wake my ancestors, their neighbors and certain historical figures, inviting them to re-enact their lives. But the roles in which I have cast them, while true to what is known about them, reach beyond their actual lives. I have challenged them to strut and fret on a larger stage, to serve as exemplars of the people of their time, and through their expanded experiences contribute to a broader understanding of the profound drama of their time, a period when the very existence of the nation and its founding principles were threatened.

Were they able to speak for themselves, I like to think they would be pleased and honored not only to be remembered by their distant progeny but also to live again through that progeny and play a role in helping the future to better understand how the drama of their lives unfolded. In some theories of mind and personal identity one could contend that they endure as a living past in subsequent generations. Through the remaining concrete evidence of their lives and minds, together with the bequeathing of their DNA, they are part of an ongoing creative process, a story still being told. It has been said, "Tell me a fact and I'll learn. Tell me a truth and I'll believe. Tell me a story and it will live in my heart forever."

It is impossible in reading about the battlefield carnage of the Civil War and the impact of the war on civilians–the neighbor against neighbor atrocities, clan hostilities and rampaging terrorists–not to see parallels between those nineteenth century horrors and the twenty first century conflict in Iraq and Afghanistan where tribes fight against each other in bloody conflict, terrorists ply their ghoulish trade, and untold civilians lose their lives. Now as then warriors and civilians, fortunate enough to survive, are both badly scarred. Now we know it as Post Traumatic Stress Disorder (PTSD). In the Civil War it was called, "Soldier's Heart."

Cambridge, Massachusetts, 2011

CHAPTER ONE

Will was stark naked. His whole body was drenched in grimy sweat mixed with smears of blood from cuts on his chest and down his arms and legs to his bare feet. He was gasping for breath and his heart was thudding furiously. He had run for what seemed like miles scrambling up rocky slopes, stumbling, sliding, tumbling head over heels down ravines, tearing his way through an endless thicket of brush and briar trying desperately to escape the enemy. With every step the tangle of branches and brambles grabbed at him, tearing off his clothes, ripping his skin. The thicket was so deep it shut out the light and its black arms snagged his right boot and pulled it off, then the left. Rifle and pistol shot set the leaves and brush around him buzzing like a thousand locusts. Cannon balls thundered into the ground on every side creating large craters, splitting whole trees in half.

All around him were dead and dying comrades. Their blood ran ankle deep and splashed up on him as he ran from the battlefield. Exhausted, he stopped and bent over at the waist, his hands on his knees, trying to catch his breath. An acrid odor filled the air and the smoke of gunpowder cast a pall over everything. As he straightened up ready to run again, the smoke swirling around him parted to reveal a huge stone wall. It reached so high into the smoky haze he could not see the top of it and it stretched far off in the distance to both his right and left.

Behind Will the sounds of onrushing infantry and cavalry and of horses pulling cannons and caissons of ammunition grew louder and louder. Will spun around to see a long line of men, some on foot, some mounted, breaking through the thicket behind him. Then they stopped and formed a semi-circle, Yankees in their pristine blue uniforms. Simultaneously they raised their rifles and pistols, all pointing at him together with a dozen or more cannons dispersed along the line of men and horses. Suddenly everything went totally silent. As the mind will do in its bizarre ways, Will thought in that instant, "those cannons are all twelve pound Napoleons." The gaping circumference of their mouths looked as big as water buckets. Both Will and the host facing him stood like frozen pieces on a hideously imbalanced chess board waiting for the chess master to decide his final move. Will instinctively bent forward slightly at the waist and covered his privates with crossed hands.

From somewhere—it seemed like in the sky above—a voice of great authority shouted "FIRE." Every pistol, every rifle and all the cannons fired simultaneously, but all the projectiles flew toward him in slow motion, a wall of bullets and cannon balls gliding through the air. On the black twelve pound ball flying at him from the center of the line he could see a name printed in bold white letters, "Willy Webb." He threw up his arms to ward it off and shouted, "No! No! My name is Will! My name is Will!"

Will's flailing arm stuck Eliza hard across the face and he could hear her voice, first through the sound of the dreadful blast, then closer, right in his ear. "Will! Wake up! Wake up!" Eliza shouted shaking him hard, "The Devil's got you again!" He leaned forward propping himself up on his elbows struggling to rise up out of the depths of his dream, but the dream was still more real than the bedroom around him and he feared falling back into it. Still bleary, his night shirt drenched in sweat, he swung his legs around and sat up on the side of the bed. The cold floor shocked his bare feet. What eventually brought him fully awake was the feel of the coarse rope behind his calves. The rope came in and out through the wooden frame of the bed along its length providing suspension for the mattress.

Will had made the bed as a wedding gift for Eliza. He had crafted it from solid walnut and gave no thought to the expense. Samantha, his first wife, had died in childbirth in the bed which they bought when they arrived from Texas and moved into their Missouri cabin. Eliza had not expressed any misgivings, but Will thought it not fitting to expect his new wife to sleep in the bed where his first wife had died.

Exhausted from the turmoil of his dream and still shaky, Will was aware now that Eliza had left their bed. She was only in the next room but she couldn't have been more distant if she had been a thousand miles away. It was a scene that had played out far too many times in the last few months and with each event Eliza had moved further away from him.

The headaches, outbursts of temper, and the nightmares that plagued Will after the war when he took up civilian life again in Texas had become less frequent after his marriage to Samantha and the birth of Lilly and Annie, but when Samantha died giving birth to their third daughter, Alta, shortly after their arrival back in Missouri, the horrors began again. He was only thirty but he felt like a worn out old man, beaten and battered by life, unable to shake off the memories and mental damage of war.

For Will the trauma of war was like a wound that wouldn't heal. His experience of life was so different from those who either escaped the war or were too young to have any memory of it that, when it was over and he tried to take up civilian life again, he felt like an imposter in his own country. The chasm was so wide that there was no point in trying to describe what happened to him and how he felt about it. Like many other warriors come home, he quickly learned that some things were best left unspoken.

Death, in the ambiguous ways it affects survivors, had brought Eliza, the love of his teenage years, back into his life. In a tragic parallel to his own life, her spouse, John Jameson, had also died after they returned from Texas, leaving her with a young daughter and son.

Will and Eliza married only nine months after Samantha died. Their first year was blissful. Their teenage desires and longings, swept away by the war, had been fulfilled beyond anything either of them had ever dared to hope in the inter-vening years. Their marriage, a simple stand-up-before-a-preacher event a week before Christmas, 1876, took on a special glow from the holiday festivities. Eliza quickly became pregnant and nine months after their wedding Will's long hoped for son was born on a beautiful early autumn day. They named him Albert.

The images of the rich yellows and reds of the Ozark foliage that joyous morning, when he rode out to fetch Doc Whitworth the year before, were swept from Will's still foggy mind by the sound of a quarrel between Eliza and her seven-year-old step-daughter, Lilly. He pulled on his boots and emerged from their bedroom, still in his long sweaty night shirt. Lilly, tall for seven, and Eliza stood face to face, their bodies stiff in anger. Annie, now four, had been quick to accept Eliza as her new mother, but Lilly was still grieving for Samantha and was not happy with the thought of this new woman taking her place.

A quick glance from Eliza told Will not to intervene. The growing trouble between Lilly and her step-mother only increased the sense of alienation from Eliza that he was feeling more and more in the wake of his troubled days and incessant nightmares. Will went back to the bedroom, dressed, and came back out hoping that the routine of break-fast would somehow help the three of them get past the moment. He knew that the tense beginning would pass and the day would eventually move on, but Will had a strong sense that it was not just another bad moment in an increas-ingly troubled marriage. He feared a corner had been turned that morning when Eliza stormed out of the bedroom.

After breakfast Will walked out through the morning sun to his shop in the barn behind their cabin, but neither the brightness of the day's beginning nor the cheery call of the neighborhood cardinal high in the tree next to his barn could dispel his gloom. Work, Will thought, will help. He stoked up the forge and began work to finish up some replacement iron fittings he had promised for Doc Whitworth's buggy that morning, but his nightmares kept replaying in his mind, distracting him from the work at hand. With the first blow to a hot iron strap on his anvil, it slipped from his tongs and flipped across his forearm, searing it badly. He ran to the bucket in which hot iron was dashed to give it strength and plunged his arm in. Ordinarily Eliza was quick to find some healing balm and wrap a burn but this was not a day to ask for her help. He sat down on the bench outside his shop and fanned the burn with his other hand.

The worst of the pain was passing when Doc Whitworth pulled up in his buggy. "Good God, Will, what've you done to yourself?" he asked. Not waiting for an answer, he pulled his worn black bag down off the seat, wet some gauze with well water to clean the wound, gently applied some salve and covered it with a bandage. During this process the men looked back and forth at each other but said nothing. Finally Doc straightened up from his work, said "Well?" and waited for an answer.

For Will the question was larger than how he burned himself. It lay inside the penumbra of all the events of the morning and was for him only a small part of the pain he felt. "Just let an iron bracket get away from me," he replied. The rest of his pain was the kind of thing he found it very difficult to talk about with anyone.

Dr. David M. Whitworth, whom everyone called "Doc," had known Will since he was a boy. Both his family and the Webb family had come to Missouri from Overton County, Tennessee, and like them his family line reached well back into colonial Virginia. Doc had studied medicine in Tennessee and came to Missouri two years after the war. He was old enough to be Will's father, but the war years had not aged him like they had Will. He spoke with the same Smoky Mountain accent but in the course of his education some of the rough edges had been polished. Like Will, he had grown up in a slave culture and like him he loved horses. Besides the mare that pulled his buggy around the county, Doc owned a Tennessee Walkin' horse. It had a splendid gait and was as fine as any riding horse in the area.

Doc instinctively knew the matter was more than a blacksmith's burn. When he spoke with Will a week earlier about repairing his buggy he had sensed then that Will was troubled. Just two years earlier, on a bitter March night, he had stood outside Will and Samantha's cabin with his arm around Will's shoulder trying to console him. Samantha had died that night giving birth to their third child. They were just settling in after returning from Texas, where Will had gone after the war. Their first two children, born in Texas, were girls and Will hadn't hidden his hope that the newborn Missouri baby would be a boy. It was a girl, and following Samantha's wishes, Will named her Alta.

Although Will had never talked to Doc about his years at war, it didn't take much imagination to understand that all the fighting and bloodshed had taken a heavy toll on the boy who went off to fight when he was only fifteen. Only two years before the war began, both of Will's parents had died of typhoid on the same day. Doc had come to Missouri several years after that tragedy but he knew that, had he been there, there was little he could have done. When typhoid struck there was little recourse beyond hope and prayer. It had struck Will too and had he not been young and strong it would have taken him as well.

Doc hoped that, when Will and Eliza married less than a year after Samantha's death, they would help each other heal from the loss of their spouses and would nurture each other's children. For Will, who had been struggling to get his blacksmith business started, it was urgent for him to find a mother for his three girls. The turmoil of the life of these two young parents and their need for healing was a condition that applied to most of the families in Jasper County. It preceded the war in the years of terror along the Missouri-Kansas border and it continued well into the 1870's as people from the county who, depending on their allegiances, had fled to Kansas or Texas, began to return to their former homes and farms.

"You should take off work for the day, Will," Doc said. "Come down to my place this afternoon and I'll give you some cream to put on that burn. You'll want to keep it on for the next few days." It was not the guidance of the town doctor but an invitation from an old family friend who hoped that a visit to his office would provide an occasion for something more than casual talk. Doc Whitworth was not an especially subtle man, so it was obvious to Will that such an invitation had little to do with salve for a burn. It was not until late in the afternoon that he decided to go. When Will knocked on Doc Whitworth's door he heard a voice from the backroom, "Come on in. Be there in a minute."

The doctor's office was in the front of his home and had a friendly feel to it that matched his approach to medicine. Will, who had been to Doc's house a number of times when his girls were sick and during Samantha's pregnancy, was always impressed by the shelves full of books in the sitting room. On the table next to Doc's reading chair was a book with a marker just inside the cover. Will slid it around so he could read the title, *The Origin of Species*. Doc had come up behind him and when he spoke he startled Will.

Being alarmed by sudden unexpected events had first become a problem for Will in the blacksmith shop in Texas after the war. More than once when a coal popped in the hearth behind him he had spun around reaching for a pistol that was not on his hip. Meeting up close with someone unexpectedly when he turned a corner was alarming in the same way. Samantha was understanding about his nervousness and that helped, but Eliza was less patient and it seemed to bring out the worst in him. More than once when Eliza surprised him from behind Will had shouted, "Don't do that!" before he could think.

Both Doc and Will pretended that there had been no awkward moment. Trying to get past it, Doc looked down at the book that had interested Will and said, "Book one of my friends back East tells me everyone is readin'. Some college professor says it's the most important book in many a year. Others say that Mr. Darwin, who wrote it, is in league with the Devil. Figured I'd best see for myself. You can borrow it if you like."

Will spun the book back around as quickly as if it had been a hot potato. "Thanks but no thanks, Doc. Don't find time to read anything much these days but my Bible." Will in fact had never been much of a reader. In such free time as he had he liked to play his fiddle.

Will had cleaned up, changed out of his work clothes and put on his Sunday-go-to-meetin' boots. Doc turned his oak swivel chair around facing away from his roll top desk, slid his reading glasses down on his nose and said, "Sit yourself down, Will." He reached to one side, slid open a bottom drawer in the desk and pulled out a half-full bottle of whiskey and two glasses. Without inquiring whether Will wanted to join him, he poured two fingers into each glass, handed one to Will, raised his and said with a smile, "To all blacksmiths and their burns."

A short silence followed that tugged each man toward some comment. As he usually did in such moments, Doc went first. He was not inclined to look for complicated reasons why people did what they did but, if he had been, he would have wondered if Will's burn was a self-inflicted cry for help. Neither man engaged much in such mental mining, Will far less than Doc. The comment he came up with was awkward but it got them started. "You're not a man, Will, to let a piece of iron right out of the coals jump up and bite him. Your mind musta been elsewhere."

Will had deliberated all through the afternoon about opening up to Doc but he had come this far, was not given to backing out of difficult situations, and there was no one in town he trusted more. He said, "I guess you're right. My mind wasn't on my work. Lately it's been all over the place, especially when I fall asleep." Will then described the dream from which he awoke that morning. He explained that his recurring nightmares began shortly after he parted company with Colonel Jo Shelby's Brigade at the end of the war and started a new life in Texas. Once he got started the stories of his years of mental anguish rolled out—the sleepless nights, headaches, jumpiness, uncharacteristic shortness of temper, and the horrific nightmares that took him back into the center of bloody battles.

Doc knew that Will's first wife, Samantha, was a gentle, caring young woman and was not surprised when Will explained that, although his behavior often frightened her, she had the patience of an older more worldly-wise woman. When their first daughter was born two years after their marriage, life began to level out. But when Samantha died so young and unexpectedly, Will's problems returned with a vengeance. His distress was so bad that Will had strong misgivings about whether a second marriage could survive it.

Like most people in the county, Doc knew the Vivion family and had heard the many tales about Eliza Vivion, the teenage Confederate spy girl, but did not know that she and Will had met back then but lost each other midway through the war.

Will stopped at that point, took a second sip of whiskey and felt more comfortable with such talk than he had been since his days in Texas when he often confided in his old blacksmith mentor, Solomon. He explained, "Eliza and I both took a chance, after being separated for ten years by the war and still grieving the loss of our spouses. It was wonderful through the first year." Feeling a little embarrassed with where he was headed, he added, "One thing, then another and Eliza got pregnant. I don't fully know why, but things started downhill then. All the bad stuff came back on me, especially the nightmares. Last night was one of the worst."

Will's mother had drilled into him when he was a boy that "men do not hit women" so the next words were the hardest of all. "I was flailing about in my night terrors in the wee hours this morning and hit Eliza hard. It wasn't the first time."

With that painful admission Will stopped, glad that he had shared it all with Doc. That relief itself would have been enough, but Doc took off his glasses, laid them on his desk and said, "You're not the only one who went to war and came back home with some nasty baggage."

Doc explained that he had recently heard from an old medical school friend who had set up practice back east in Philadelphia. He took some papers from a compartment in the top of his desk, laid them down beside him without looking at them and shared what he had learned from studies of the experience of a group of Civil War veterans.

"All of the mental anguish you have just described, and more, was laid out by a Doctor, name of Jacob De Costa. He was workin' at the Soldier's Home in Philadelphia and became concerned with how many men, years after the war, had great trouble gettin' their lives back together. Especially troublin' was the high number of suicides among Pennsylvania veterans and others across the country."

"To make a long story short, in 1871 he studied the post war lives of nearly two hundred veterans of the battle of Gettysburg." Doc put his hand flat on the papers next to him and added, "My friend sent me this report which Da Costa presented to a medical convention. He found that the troubles for veterans usually began within three months after they left the service but in many cases continued for years later. When you described your own experiences just now it could have come right out of the doctor's study."

Behind Doc was a window full of the setting sun. He looked like a black cutout surrounded by a warm golden glow as he continued, "Sounds, smells and images triggered flashbacks and night terrors in which the veterans relived wartime events. Episodes of racin' hearts, rapid breathin' and bad sweats could last minutes or even hours. A kind of mental numbness often set in, punctuated by periods of sudden and unprovoked irritability and anger. They often lay awake for hours tryin' to fall asleep. When they remembered the deaths of friends they felt guilty that they'd survived. The pleasures of life were hard to come by and often it was hard for them to do any productive work beyond routine things."

Will had been swept up in Doc's account. His own experiences wove in and out of the details as Doc spoke. Taken back into his own experience, his heart was racing and he had broken out in sweat. Gathering himself he said, "That's me, Doc. That's me for sure. All that and more."

"They have a name for it, Will," Doc said, "It's called 'Soldier's Heart'." For himself, he often thought that just giving a name to some malady, especially in Latin as the medical profession often did, contributed little or nothing to real healing, but it was obvious that it meant something to Will—not just that his experience had a name but that he was not alone in what the war did to him. He was not going crazy.

Will was still absorbing the moment when Doc said, "I guess you could say, Will, that there is more than one kind of burn. Some things can singe the heart. And there is no miracle cream that can heal that kind of damage. Only time. I think you know that I'm always here if talkin' more about these things would help."

Everyone around knew that Doc was an intellectual kind of man. He read a lot of books and knew a lot of history and literature, so it didn't surprise Will as he stood to go home that Doc offered a parting piece of wisdom, "Maybe the beginnin' of your heart's healing will be tonight when you go to bed. Like Shakespeare said, 'Sleep knits up the raveled sleeve of care.'"

Will was halfway out the door when Doc called him back and handed him a small white jar. "You forgot your cream, Will."

At home there was no forgetting how the morning began. Eliza had little to say beyond what was necessary to get through supper and see the children off to bed. She went to bed early without a word and lay with her face to the wall. Later when Will slid in beside her he could, without touching her, feel the warmth emanating from her body but the bed was cold with alienation. She might as well have been all the way back in colonial Virginia where her Huguenot ancestors fled to escape persecution in France.

Sleep came to him with difficulty, but for that night at least there were no violent nightmares. He dreamed that Doc Whitworth had him take off his shirt and lie on an examination table. Doc was still a black cut-out with the golden glow behind him. From a large white jar he took some cream that shone with the same glow and rubbed it on Will's chest. He could feel it penetrating his skin and flowing in around his heart, warming it, soothing it. It was the kind of dream one wants to slip back into when one begins to wake but Will could not recapture it.

When he came out of the bedroom Eliza was sitting in the rocking chair nursing Albert, the baby boy who should have secured their union. To Will it was always the best image of parenthood, but when Eliza finally looked up at him and spoke the image was shattered. "I'm leavin', Will," she said abruptly.

"Leavin'?" he puzzled.

"Leavin'. I'm goin' home. Mother is making a place for me and the children." And by children it was clear with Albert suckling at her breast that she meant not only Mary and William, her children by John Jameson, but also Will's only son, Albert. Things had never been easy with Eliza's mother Julia. The bond between mother and daughter was unusually strong. Five years before the war Julia's husband had been trampled by a team of mules in a bizarre farm accident. Eliza was only eight at the time, but she became her mother's main support and Julia never remarried.

When the war began the county erupted around them. Like many of their neighbors caught up in guerilla attacks and fierce Union reaction they feared for their lives and fled in haste to safety in Texas—just the two of them in a wagon that carried the few things they could pack into it. After the war Julia returned to reclaim her farm and set up a place for Eliza to come back to with her husband and children. The death of Eliza's young husband shortly after they returned brought mother and daughter even closer.

When Will began courting Eliza a few months later, Julia made it clear she did not want him coming round, and when he and Eliza married a week before Christmas in '76, it was over Julia's objections. At first Will thought he could bring her around. He had seen enough of the impact of the war on civilians to sympathize with what she had gone through— more tragedy on top of becoming a widow with young children to raise. Will began to think Julia saw promise in him but that changed when Eliza announced her pregnancy. In various ways, both direct and indirect, Julia began to place herself between them. To her Will became more an intruder than a son-in-law.

It became impossible for Will to have a serious conversation with Julia, so he never fully understood the reasons for her hostility. He had heard the gossip that Julia first accepted him because she thought he would become wealthy as a result of lead ore being found on Webb family land. When it became clear that was not going to happen, as the rumors had it, Julia laid her plans to reclaim Eliza and her grandchildren–all of them. More than once in his life Will had been accused of being too ready to think the best of people, but even if there was some truth in what people said about Julia, he was confident that was not why Eliza married him. The powerful attraction they felt for each other happened early in the war, a decade before Will's older brother, J.C., found lead on the family land.

These thoughts raced through Will's mind in the seconds after Eliza declared her plans. "For how long?" Will said. His words hung in the air unanswered long enough for him to anticipate the worst.

When Eliza finally responded her voice was more subdued than with her first announcement. She looked down at the baby, blissfully unaware that his life was at that moment taking a dramatic turn, and said softly, "I don't know, Will. Until. Until."

He felt a strong surge of the "you can't do that" kind of anger but suppressed it. In such moments he often heard his mother speaking in his mind, quoting from the Bible one of the many verses she helped him and his siblings commit to memory, "A soft answer turneth away wrath, but grievous words stir up anger." His answer went beyond softness. It was unspoken, delayed until he could find a better moment.

Two uncertain weeks followed as Eliza made her arrangements and the better moment for Will to speak was pushed forward into an uncertain future. Even as a teenager Eliza lived life with determination once she made a decision and, unbeknownst to Will, it was for her more than just a separation. Whether it was her decision alone or not, she had already met with a lawyer and that was a prelude to grievous words and anger.

Packing their wagon with her belongings took up most of the morning on the day Eliza left. Her son, young William, sat in the back astride a trunk and Mary sat beside her mother holding baby Albert. William, who had developed an affection for his step-father and loved pumping the forge bellows, waved goodbye. As Eliza with a "walk on" to the team swung the wagon around heading west, the side with Mary holding Albert brushed Will back. Little Albert's tiny bare feet were pressing against the front board of the wagon. That innocent image slightly softened the sad moment. "Such long toes for such little feet," Will thought.

The days that followed Eliza's departure were a numbing succession of gray mornings and evenings. Will thought of Doc's quote from Shakespeare, but instead of being knitted up the raveled sleeve of care was now falling into tatters. His older brother Ben's wife, Jane, had taken in his frail younger brother, Eli, during the war years and now offered to take in his three girls for a few weeks to allow him to focus on the increasing volume of work coming to his blacksmith shop and get things settled with Eliza.

The girls loved their Aunt Jane and Will knew she would take good care of them, but when he took them over to Ben's farm he was shocked to see how much his brother had wasted away in the three weeks since he last saw him. Ben had consumption. He had lost so much weight his face had the look of a thinly covered skull and his eyes were sinking into the dark hollows of death. They exchanged the usual brotherly banter and friendly insults but it was awkward. Both felt the wordless communication that underlay their teasing, grave communication. Jane busied herself with the girls and their things, but her occasional glance at Will filled in her part of the silent communication.

The buggy ride back home felt longer than the trip over and it seemed that his young dapple mare was straining as though pulling a heavier load home, even though the buggy was now three persons and a load of baggage lighter. When Will opened the barn door he was surprised not to see Circus' big black head over his stall door, snorting a greeting. He was lying on his side in the straw breathing a slow shallow breath. Will closed the barn door, leaving the mare still hitched to the buggy. He opened the stall door and sat down in the straw beside Circus. The old black stallion, now grey in the muzzle, tried but could not raise his head. His only greeting was an eye turned toward Will.

It was not as though Will hadn't seen the warning signs of Circus' decline. His neighbors and customers, who learned he had come from Tennessee as a colt before the Civil War, often remarked about how a horse could live so long. But as it is with what one loves in life, the inevitable always defies expectation. Will's life had in some respects been measured out by the life of his horse. Their days had been days together—from the comfort Will had found in Circus when grieving as a boy for the loss of both of his parents, through the fury and horror of the war years. They travelled the long road down to exile in Texas and 10 years later back home to Missouri, but their journey together had now ended and it was clear what had to be done. Will took his Henry rifle from the storage room in the barn, swung the lever to cock it, waited for Circus to turn his eye from him and fired.

The sound of rifle shot and acrid smell of gunsmoke hung in the air as Will, standing in the rear corner of the stall, slid slowly down, sitting with his back to the wall. The grim despair that had been building steadily since Eliza announced she was leaving, taking his only son with her, now totally engulfed him smothering all hope and reason. Will cocked the rifle again, put the butt between his boots and the barrel under his chin.

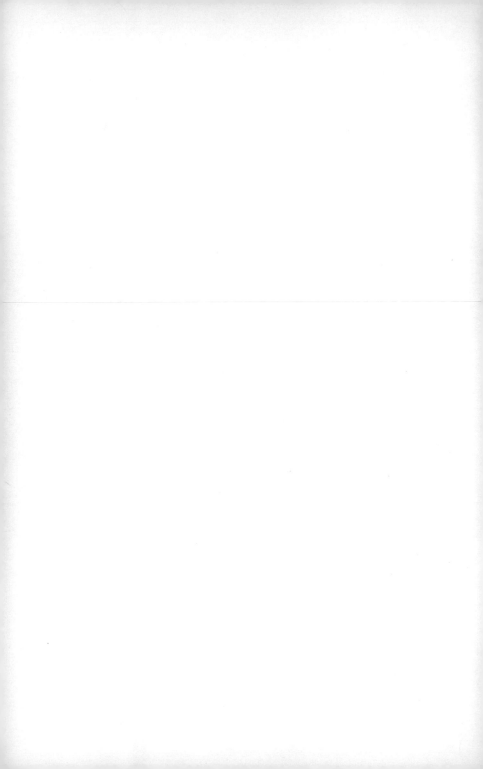

CHAPTER TWO

Six young bare feet dangled from the barn loft of Elijah Webb's Overton, Tennessee farm. The two feet on the left and the two on the right were white. The two in the middle were brown. Below them a hectic drama was being played out. Like a bootless short pants version of a classical Greek chorus the three boys, perched high above the noisy stage, heckled the dramatic action below and called out their boyish criticisms of how things were being done. The players in the dusty commotion beneath them were a mix of members of the extended Webb clan and the more than two dozen slaves of the family patriarch, Elijah. They were finishing up two months of preparation for a several hundred mile journey. It was the early autumn of 1856 and they wanted to arrive at their destination in southwest Missouri before winter set in.

Elijah was descended from a wealthy family of Virginia slave owners which dated back to the mid 1600's and traced their roots across the Atlantic to Gloucestershire, England. His branch of the Webb family had struck out over the Appalachians into eastern Tennessee and after a number of years there, like quite a few of their neighbors, they were on the move further west to what they judged were more promising lands. One of Elijah's brothers had gone ahead of them a couple of years earlier and had written back glowingly of the prospects.

The two long and slender loft feet on the right belonged to ten year old William James Webb, the next to the youngest of Elijah's five sons, whom everyone called Willy. The two on the far left belonged to Willy's brother, the youngest son who was named after his father but was called Eli. The two brown feet in the middle belonged to Micah, whose age lay some uncertain months between Willy and Eli. Micah had been their friend and constant playmate as long as they could remember. That he was also owned by their father didn't register much with them, nor did what they had heard of how that kind of property arrangement stretched back for more than two hundred years in the family. It was for them just the way things were–like the sun rising every morning and setting every evening.

What none of the three boys knew that morning was that at an auction the previous week in nearby Livingston, one of the county's larger towns, the Webbs had sold a number of their slaves. They had cut down their holdings to twenty-three. Each of those kept was judged to be fit for the long trip and essential to the family and farming in Missouri. Micah and the grandmother who cared for him, old

Edna, would be staying behind, but they had not yet learned that.

The swirl and bustle of the activity below—men, women, children, the animals of the farm, and slaves of all ages—made Willy think of the carnivals that came to the county seat, stirred up a lot of excitement for a few days, then struck their tents, packed up and moved on to another town. Peter, the family's oldest slave, could have been the carnival's strong man. He was over six feet tall with a muscular build. Willy had once seen him lift up the back corner of a wagon by himself so a new wheel could be put on. To Willy, Peter stood out among the family's slaves who all saw him as their leader. He carried himself with dignity and often displayed a special knowledge of things.

There was no bearded lady, but one of Willy's aunts had a faint mustache. And where was the clown? There was, along with the excitement and sense of adventure, also a certain sadness about leaving home for some unknown place hundreds of miles away. A clown would have helped.

Why the family was moving was not completely clear to Willy. His uncle, James Crittendon Webb, had already moved to Missouri and urged his relatives to come up and buy land near his farm. After a trip up to see for himself, Willy's oldest brother, John Cornwall, who preferred to be called J.C., came back convinced that the whole family should move there. He and Elijah's next oldest son, Ben, had bought a large tract of Missouri land. Willy assumed that life there would be farming like their lives in Tennessee, but he had also heard his father and older brothers discussing other mysterious prospects. It had to do with what they called the "shines." J.C., who was the most enthusiastic about new opportunities in Missouri, from his last visit there, had brought back samples of glistening rocks with square edges and cubic protrusions. He believed there might be great riches lying under the Missouri soil.

J.C. was twenty years older than Will and saw himself as the eventual heir to the title of patriarch of the Webb clan. To him, the youngest boys in the family, James, Willy and Eli, were mostly nuisance children. To them, J.C. was a self-appointed, undesired and bossy second father. They also were not very fond of J.C.'s son, Elijah Thomas. Imitating his father, he liked to be called by his initials, E.T., but to Willy, James, and Eli he was just plain Tom. Some in the family were more inclined to refer to him as "spoiled Tom."

J.C.'s packed wagon and buckboard had been brought over from his nearby farm the night before to be ready for an early departure. He had returned home that night to finish up the paper work with the family who had bought his farm. The boys in the loft watched as J.C. came at a gallop out of the strand of trees that separated his land from his father's. J.C. rode straight through the gaggle of men, women, children, animals and slaves, scattering them in every direction. They heard him shout to no one in particular, "What's goin' on here? We all agreed we'd roll out right after sun up." No one in particular answered him, and that was not an uncommon occurrence. Ben and Paulina, the siblings nearest his age, were no more inclined to anoint him as patriarch-in-waiting than were James, Will, or little Eli. They did, however, share his eagerness to get the journey started.

Their mother, Martha Jane, had been less enthusiastic about leaving the comfort of their Tennessee home for a long arduous journey to the frontier of Missouri. The night before, lying awake late, Willy had heard her say to his father, "J.C. sees Missouri as some kind of Paradise. Maybe he's right, but first we have to get everyone there safe and sound." She also spoke of her concern for their daughter, Mary Ann, who had married Jesse Terry. "She's coughin' more every day and seems worn out carin' for our new grandbaby."

Fully as exciting to Willy as this new adventure, was his father's promise that the day before they left he could take his pick of their three new colts. It was to be his own horse in Missouri. With his father on one side and old Peter on the other, he had watched the three colts gamboling around in the enclosure behind the barn. Now and then they would kick up their hind legs and race off a few yards. Peter leaned down to Will and said softly, "Pick the black one, Willy. Someday he'll be growin' up a powerful fine stallion. Might make sixteen hands." Willy had learned to respect old Peter's judgment about animals and, had he favored one of the other two colts, disagreeing would not have been easy. But Willy had already made the same choice days before. For him it had to be the little black horse with the white circle on his forehead. Now he had to decide what to call him.

Elijah had been so caught up in seeing that all the last details had been attended to that the oxen had not yet been brought up to his third wagon. He layed the yoke and pinned the bow on the family's oldest ox, an ugly beast called Henry. Ned, a younger and petulant ox, shorter of leg than most, bawled and balked at his side of the yoke. It took both Elijah and James to wrestle him into place. Fatigued, James leaned against the wagon and said, "I'd just as soon yoke up a buffalo as that damned ox." Elijah nodded agreement but shot a glance that reminded James how he felt about swearing.

Elijah's three wagons were packed so full that, had they been carnival wagons, there would have been no space available for the fat lady. Juliette, one of Willy's middle sisters, was not fat but her second trunk was. It was stuffed full of dresses that she had refused to winnow down to a reasonable number. She sat on top of it pouting after her father had said there was simply no more room for it and noted that she had already used up more than her fair share of wagon space. Tearing up she argued that her second trunk was more important than the last box her father had just loaded into the third wagon. "You'd take that old junk but not my best dresses?"

"The trunk stays," said Elijah. "Pick out one dress to go with all the others you've already packed and jam it in wherever you can. The 'old junk', as you call it, might just save our lives. It's a box of extra brake shoes. You'll feel different about such junk the first time we reach the top of a steep hill and look way down the other side."

Following Elijah's wagons and buckboard was J.C.'s wagon. Jabez Hatcher, who had married Will's oldest sister Paulina, was next in line. At the end of the caravan were the wagons of two other kinfolk. In all there were seven covered wagons and assorted other small buckboards. Tied behind some were milk cows. Some of the men drove the wagons and others rode their horses. Behind Elijah's third wagon Willy had tied his colt. He planned to walk all the way to Missouri beside him.

The women and little children settled into their places in the wagons. The slaves walked. They had no choice. It was only when the caravan was ready to leave that Willy realized that Micah was not coming. He was standing barefoot in the center of a group of former slaves and neighbors beside the road. Old Edna was holding him tightly to keep him from running after Willy. Impulsively, Willy jumped up into the back of the wagon, dug into a bag of his clothes, grabbed a pair of his brogans, tied their laces together and flung them out to Micah. It was only as they sailed through the air that he realized they were his Sunday-go-ta-meetin' shoes. As Micah picked them up and waived goodbye to Willy with them, Elijah's voice booming voice broke through the moment, "Move 'em out!"

In the odd fashion that moments in life sometimes connect in bizarre ways, Willy was reminded that his mother had given Micah his name from one of her favorite books of the Bible and he remembered a passage from it that she had insisted all her children memorize, "And what doth the Lord require of thee but to do justly, love mercy, and walk humbly with thy God." Young Micah, his friend, would always have to walk humbly but, Willy thought, he would do it in some new shoes.

James came up beside Willy laughing at their father's corny wagon master command. Looking back at the long curving line of people and their possessions, he said, "Look, Willy. What a sight. A body might judge we're a ragtag army gearing up to invade Mizzoury."

Every man in the Webb clan had more than one gun and Willy had heard talk of marauding Indians, but joining up with an army didn't appeal much to him. He preferred the image of a carnival caravan seeking out new towns where they would delight the natives and make them laugh. He was running away with the circus and it occurred to him that in James, he now had his clown.

Willy couldn't remember the last time he was as tired as when the caravan stopped that first day out. Elijah reckoned they had made twenty-five miles or more. It didn't seem like much progress on such a long trip, but Willy was glad he didn't have to walk another step. He might have been tempted to complain, had he not thought about what the day must have been like for their slaves. Half or more of them were barefoot. And he wondered about his little black colt. His father had told him to check his hoofs for cracks and fill up any he found with tar.

After the first supper out on the trail, the men gathered around the campfire, puffed on their corncob pipes and tried to one-up each other about who had the biggest hardships of the day. J.C., full of his opinions as always, cut through the men's banter. He reminded everyone that he had already made one trip up to Missouri. "Hard day?" he laughed. "Wait'il you see what's in store for us up ahead. We've gotta drag these wagons over some mighty big hills and after that it's crossin' the Ohio, even worse the Mississippi."

From Overton County west to Nashville each of the next several days was pretty much like the other. One day an iron wheel on someone's wagon needed repair. Another day the pin on an oxen yoke broke. Then there was the rain, which came down so hard on two days, that everyone had to take shelter for a few hours. The wagons at the back of the caravan found it much tougher going than those in the lead, bogging down in the muddy ruts cut through ahead of them.

Things were difficult enough on level ground but steep grades, greased by the rain, frightened even the most courageous among them. Willy tried very hard to be as brave as the grown men and, even though he was only ten, on some days he felt pretty manly.

The night their party camped out to the west of Nashville was a turning point for Willy. The women were clearing up after the meal and the men had gathered to smoke and chew the fat as they did each night, when suddenly out of the dark a big bear of a man appeared. Willy had never seen anything like him. He was well over six feet tall and wore a broad brimmed hat with feathers stuck in the hat band. His beard was dirty red and his hair hung down on his shoulders. His tight fitting clothes were made of tanned skins that were fringed down his arms and legs. Willy could see from the campfire that his horse was a pinto and on a line behind him was a heavily packed donkey.

With an accent, that sounded a bit British and was at odds with his appearance, the stranger said, "My apologies if I startled you folks. I'm wonderin' if I could join up with you for a piece? I know this trail west and perhaps can be of use to you." Willy didn't often hear people use the word "perhaps."

It took a while for the men in the clan to figure out a response to such an abrupt appearance and request. Elijah, the first to speak, said "Sit yourself down. Reckon you might like some coffee." That began an hour of back and forth in which Willy, listening intently, learned that their visitor was called a "Mountain Man," that he had spent more than a decade travelling through the western wilderness hunting, trapping and trading. His father, he explained, was an English adventurer. His mother was Cherokee, the daughter of a medicine man. The Cherokees gave him his first name, "Swims Swift Water," and he took his last name, "Randolph," from his father. Before it was time to bed down there was an unspoken consensus among the caravan men that this Mountain Man could be trusted and in fact had knowledge of the route west that might be very useful. What filled Willy's mind as he curled up in his bedroll was not how this mysterious man could be of use on the trail, but what he could learn about adventures in the wilderness, what a medicine man was, and above all how he got his unusual first name.

When the wagon train stopped for a break at noon the next day, Willy sat down beside the Mountain Man who, instead of putting his behind on the ground, squatted and leaned his back against a tree. Willy peppered him with questions, starting with his name.

The Mountain Man raised himself up and down slightly from his knees scratching his back on the tree and said, "As a boy I lived with my mother among the Cherokees. Only saw my father now and then when he came back from his trapping and trading trips. When I was about your age, a small boy and I were playing beside a stream when he fell in. The rushing water swept him away and I dove in, was able somehow to reach him and dragged him out. That night my grandfather called me to his tent and told me my name from that day on would "Swims Swift Water." It's a mouth full and makes no sense in Cherokee to white men, so mostly I'm called 'Randolph.'"

It was obvious to Willy that tale was all he was going to get that day from Randolph, but he knew what his next question would be. He had over heard him talking with his father, Elijah, earlier that morning about heading west out of Tennessee along a route called "The Trail of Tears."

During the next few days the wagon train rolled west across the northwest corner of Tennessee into the southwest corner of Kentucky. The hills grew steeper by the day slowing progress, but as the clan moved farther and farther away from the comfort and safety of home, what was on everyone's mind, but largely unspoken, was fear of being attacked by Indians. Carried away by their imaginations, the children often claimed they saw Indians in the woods beyond the trail. Willy's sister, Annie, who was two years younger than he, saw redskin danger so often that everyone scoffed at her. On the second day into Kentucky Annie, who was walking beside Willy, pointed off to the right of the trail and shouted, "Look, Willy!"

Willy thought he also saw a figure ride away into the brush. The next day, as the lead wagons pulled out of a long bend in the trail, there on a cliff high above were four Indians on their ponies. They were standing so still they could have been statues. The first instinct of all of the men was to reach for their rifles, but the Mountain Man shouted back down the line, "No shooting." By the time he turned back around the Indians were gone. For the first time that night the wagons were arranged in a circle.

Early the next afternoon the Indians reappeared and for an hour or more moved through the woods parallel to the wagon train's route. Fear slowly turned into curiosity. Some of the younger children dared to wave. When a stop was made to rest the animals, one of the Indians rode halfway toward the wagons then stopped. Elijah and the Mountain

Man huddled together for a few minutes then together walked up toward the Indian. Everyone in the back wagons came forward to see what was going on. The women gathered together with the children and the men stood in front of them in a line holding their rifles barrel down. It appeared a lively conversation was going on up the hill. The Indian leader pointed down at the wagon train several times. Finally Elijah and Randolph, who had served as translator, walked back to the wagon train and everyone gathered around them.

Elijah spoke to his daughter, Juliette. "Looks like you have charmed him, dear. He fancies your red hair." Then after a teasing pause he added, "Oh no, not for a scalp. He thinks you'd make a fine squaw."

Juliette ran to her mother and bawled, "His squaw? Mother!"

Elijah waited longer than he should have then added, "We almost made a trade, but when I told him how few dresses you had, he grunted something which Randolph translated, "No deal."

When Juliette ran at her father and pounded him in the chest he added for all to hear, "What he really wanted was Willy's black colt." It was clear that Elijah was not in a trading mood, but had he been, Willy thought to himself, "They'd have had to trade me too. No one's gonna separate me from my horse."

That night the campfire discussion was about Indians with everyone asking the Mountain Man about what the real dangers were. A jug of whiskey lubricated the jawing. Randolph, who clearly liked to see himself as a source of wisdom, painted a frightening picture, "Where you folks are goin', up in Mizzoury, it ain't Indians you need to worry about. Last time I passed through there, the white men were raisin' all kinds of hell along the border with Kansas."

"There's what they call 'Jayhawkers' on one side and 'Bushwackers' on the other. They're carousin' around the countryside, mostly at night, fightin' each other, robbin', burnin' down houses, hackin' each other up. The abolitionists come over from the Kansas side and steal the white folks' Negras, then the slave owners retaliate. Cain't see the end to it."

Willy had never heard such terrible things. This couldn't be the "promised land" that they were leaving Tennessee for. Elijah had seen the distress in Willy's face and spoke to him before everyone settled in for the night. "Never you mind the Mountain Man's tales, Willy. It's the whiskey talkin'. We'll all be fine." It was what Willy needed to hear, but Elijah hadn't convinced himself.

Unfortunately the events of the following day only served to confuse Willy and heighten his fears about life in Missouri. About an hour before midday, a group men on horseback rode up alongside the wagon train. They were armed and had a number of hound dogs with them. They said they were chasing a runaway slave, a stocky built very dark Negra man who had a slight limp. Elijah assured them no such man had been seen, but the air was electric as the posse rode on ahead. The Webb's Negras talked excitedly among themselves and Willy's older brothers, along with the other men in the wagon train, sat apart talking after their noon meal. He hadn't been invited to join in that conversation but he could hear bits and pieces of what was said.

He heard J.C., who often spoke more loudly than the rest of the men, say, "Well, it's not hard to understand why they're determined to chase their runaways down. A healthy Negra male in his prime brings top money. I seen one a couple of months ago bring $2,000! For lots of families it's their most valuable possession." Willy heard one expression several times that struck him as very odd. "Underground railroad." There were, of course, many railway tunnels but how could there be a whole railroad underground?

The description of the runaway as "very dark" raised a question again in Willy's mind that had puzzled him for some time. A few of his family's Negras were very dark, some less so, and some, such as the pretty Julia and her two children, Harriet and Granville, were nearly as light-skinned as Willy. It seemed to him that there often was a difference in how slaves were treated that related to their skin color. This was especially true of Julia, Harriet and little Granville. Harriet, who was about six, and Granville, whom Willy figured was about two, seemed to get special treatment from Elijah. The children rode in Jesse Terry's wagon and their mother, Julia, didn't have to walk as much as the family's other slaves.

It had always been easy for Willy to take his questions to his mother so when he was allowed to drive the family's lead wagon for part of a day, sitting up beside his mother, he asked her why Harriet and little Granville were so much lighter than their other slaves. He was surprised by her sharp tone when she answered dismissively, "It's complicated."

Willy persisted, "Does it have to do with how much time they spend in the sun?" He had hardly gotten the last word out when his mother fixed him with a stern glance and harshly ended their conversation. "I said it's complicated, Willy." It was the same sentence as before but with the word "said" stressed and there was a look of both anger and pain in his mother's eyes that he had never seen before.

The next day the Mountain Man volunteered to drive Jesse Terry's wagon for the day and Jesse rode the pinto horse. It was much more comfortable for Willy to sit up beside Randolph than it would have been to ride another day with his mother, and anyway he wanted another chance to ask his questions. The "Trail of Tears" was at the top of the list.

"You're mighty curious, boy," the Mountain Man said, but in truth he always looked for a chance to enlighten white men about what they had done to his people and the younger they were the better, if minds were to be changed.

"For most men, Willy, all Indians are lumped together as dangerous savages who ride around on horses without saddles, hunt with bow and arrow and live in teepees. Even worse are the views of some powerful men like President Andrew Jackson who've said all Indians are vermin and what really should be done is exterminate them. At best it was claimed they're in the way of civilization. If they could be moved and confined in the wilderness lands of the west, then civilization could proceed safely."

The Mountain Man wondered how much Willy could absorb. He reached into his chest pocket, pulled out a plug of tobacco, bit off a chunk and offered Willy a chaw. Willy looked around to see who might be watching, was tempted for an instant, but declined.

"The Cherokee are a special people, Willy. Early on they saw that the way to survive as a nation was to adopt the white man's ways. They cultivated farms, built cabins, grist mills and blacksmith shops. They had schools and libraries and created their own government. Many spoke both Cherokee and English. But none of that was enough. White men in parts of the Carolinas, northern Georgia and Tennessee wanted their land. Sadly for the Cherokee, they had found gold on their land. That only whetted the white's appetite further."

Randolph spit tobacco juice in the air to his right. Willy, on his left, appeared to still be paying attention. "All hell broke loose," he continued, "when the Government set up something called the New Echota Treaty. In a word, it gave the government the right to drive the Cherokee off their land. With little or no warning men were dragged in from their fields, women were snatched out of their kitchens, children torn away from their toys. As they were hauled off, some had to watch as local white men whom they knew had looted and burned their homes. Few even had a chance to grab warm clothes. They were herded together and locked up in government stockades. Any who resisted were severely beaten or put in chains. In the holding pens some died of starvation and others of exposure and pneumonia. There were epidemics of measles and cholera."

"The death toll was horrendous, as many as four thousand. Some say that a third of all the Cherokees caught up in that tragedy died. Many died along the very trail we're on now. We'll reach the Ohio River in a few days and just east of where we cross I'll show you Mantle Rock, a place full of Cherokee ghosts. There's a large natural out- cropping over a hundred feet long and ten to twelve feet high. It forms a cave overarched with a rock shaped like a bridge. My people sheltered there against the bitter cold for several days waiting for the ice to break up on the great river. They huddled up to share their body heat with each other trying to survive. Many perished."

Most of Willy's childish thoughts about Indians were being turned upside down. He was trying hard to fight back tears when Randolph ended his tale by describing the river crossing. "The Ohio ferrymen," he explained, "took advantage of the Cherokees and bumped up their crossing fees, charging a dollar a head. Piling evil on evil, the government made them pay it out of their own pockets."

The Mountain Man punctuated his story with another spit of tobacco juice to his right. Willy was struck both by the intensity of his emotion and by the way he had with words, but he couldn't get his mind around the idea of four thousand dead Indians. He had never even seen four thousand people together in one place. When he crawled into his bedroll that night his head was still swimming with the dramatic pictures Randolph had painted. In his fitful sleep the trail to Missouri was strewn all along the way with thousands of Cherokee bodies. Many of them were children huddled together in frozen groups. Never before had Willy been so grateful for the clattering of pots and pans, and the smell of bacon, choke biscuits and trail coffee that woke him the next morning.

Elijah drafted Willy to drive the lead wagon that day. He was proud to be given such an important job, but was unaware that his father was concerned about the Mountain Man loading up his mind with troubling stories. That left James to hook up with Randolph and ask his own questions. That night James, knowing Willy would be jealous, told Willy that Randolph had told him about a great monster they might meet up with when they got to the Ohio.

"Monster, what kind of monster?" Willy said.

"It's a monster the Cherokee call Uktena," James replied. Determined to make the story as scary as he could, he added, "He looks like a great horned snake. He's as big as a tree and if you even look at him your whole family could die. Long ago he was a man who was sent to kill the sun because it had scorched the land, but he failed. He was turned into a monster and banished forever to the deep river. Years ago when the Cherokee were being driven west, they were so afraid of the monster that the soldiers had a hard time herding them onto the ferry boats for the crossing."

Two days later the wagon train arrived at Mantle Rock and made camp there for the night. It was just as Randolph described. Had he not known about what happened to the Cherokees there, it would have been a great place to explore but Willy kept his distance and that night, lying in his bedroll under the wagon with his colt tied behind, he wondered if the ghosts ever wandered out of the cave. It didn't help that his little black colt seemed fidgety.

As the wagon train rolled out the next morning the damp of the river was in the air. Cresting a hill they saw the mighty Ohio for the first time. Willy was amazed at how wide and powerful it was. Elijah had said that the wagons would go across on flatboats, but moored at the bank was a mighty mechanical giant, a steamboat freighter. Black smoke rolled out of its stacks together with the sound of hissing steam. Elijah's lead wagon went on first, followed by J.C.'s and the Hatchers. By contrast to what Randolph said the Cherokees had been forced to pay, the Webb clan was charged only twelve and a half cents per wagon.

Hoping not to draw attention to himself, Willy kept a watchful eye for the river monster all the way across. Had there been anything below them, the river was too muddy to see it. The other children, who knew nothing of the dangerous monster, ran around the boat excitedly. The animals were restless which made Willy wonder whether they detected something he couldn't sense. It took several trips to get all the wagons and buckboards across. Willy was glad to go with the first group. Perhaps Uktena was just a whiskey tale. From the security of the far bank, he watched as one by one the wagons were unloaded and hauled up through the mud to a high Illinois ridge. At the end of the day the wagon train stopped at a small town called Golconda.

Two more trouble-free days across the tip of Illinois brought the Webbs to the Mississippi. The Ohio had been wide but the Mississippi was even wider. Willy wondered how deep it was and what lay in its depths. His father had hoped there would be steamboats to carry them across, as at the Ohio, but there were only flatboats. To Willy they looked like little more than rafts. Around all four sides were rails to keep the wagons and animals from falling in. The rails at the front and rear came down to allow for loading and unloading. Each boat held two wagons and their animals.

Elijah sent Willy to the second wagon in line to help with the animals there. It was J.C.'s wagon. A handsome dapple grey mare named Lady, J.C.'s favorite horse, was put in Willy's care. She was tethered to the wagon, but Willy's assignment was to stay beside her and keep her calm during the crossing. The ferryman called the Mississippi the "Long Man," but Willy thought a better name was the "Wide Man," given how long it was taking to cross. By the time they were half way Willy was feeling less worried about river monsters. He was stroking Lady's neck when suddenly something on the upriver side struck the boat hard and tipped it high up in the air. Willy grabbed the rear wagon wheel to keep from being thrown over and looked up to see J.C.'s horse snap her tether and jump over the rail into the river. Riderless, she had no idea which way to swim and, caught in the swift current, she was beyond saving, had anyone been foolish enough to dive in after her.

Willy had been on the receiving end of J.C.'s irritation more than once but now he was seething with anger. Elijah stepped in between them, pulled Willy around behind his back and put his hand on J.C.'s chest. "You can't blame the boy, J.C." Elijah said. "There's no way he could have held onto your horse. We're lucky we didn't all go over, people and wagons together. Something really big hit us. Musta been a tree trunk three or four feet thick." His father could believe that if he wanted to, but Willy was thinking "Utkena." The three, Elijah standing between his sons, looked down river. Lady was almost out of sight.

Willy stayed clear of J.C. the rest of the way across and after they landed on the Missouri side. He knew J.C. would simmer in his anger for days and feared it might be weeks, maybe even the rest of their lives. J.C. wanted to borrow his father's horse and ride down the river bank to look for Lady but Elijah told him it was a fool's errand. "You saw how fast she was swept downstream," he said, "She'd be so far to the south by now you'd never catch up with her and we gotta keep moving west."

At the nightly gathering of the men, they poured over Elijah's crude maps. He said, "I reckon we've made it more than half way. God willin', we should be there in a fortnight or less." Willy thought that God must surely have been willing. He had saved them from the monster Uktena.

It had almost become an evening routine for the Mountain Man to entertain with his stories. But before he could begin that night Elijah raised a question that had been on several people's minds. "You speak with great ease, Randolph, and know a lot of words that most of us don't use or have never heard before. Seems to me you musta had some good schoolin' along the way."

"Indeed I did." Randolph responded with a flourish. He put his hand on Willy's shoulder and said, "When I was about the age of this young'un, my father learned that he had inherited the family estate in England. After long discussions with my mother and her father, it was decided that I should go back across the ocean with him where I could get a proper education. Schoolin' in the ways of the white man was very important to the Cherokees, so this looked like an opportunity that shouldn't be passed up."

"No one consulted me," Randolph continued, "And had I known how seasick I would be for weeks during the Atlantic crossing, I would have objected to the whole idea." Adept at gauging his audience's attention, Randolph continued, "After a long coach ride from Portsmouth we reached Grantham, the town in the middle of England nearest the Randolph family estate. Where I was to live was a far cry from a teepee. Surrounded by hundreds of acres of land was what they called a Manor House. To me it looked more like a castle."

"Well, to make a long story short I was enrolled in Kings School, a centuries old boy's grammar school in Grantham, and spent several years there. I was the school's curiosity and the butt of a lot of bad jokes. My Indian name was shortened by my classmates to "Swifty." I was taught history and maths, learned to speak and write English properly and studied French, Greek and Latin. One of the boys, a couple hundred years ahead of me at Kings, grew up to be a genius scientist and mathematician." He looked down at Willy who was hanging on every word and added, "I'll tell you about him someday and what he learned from a fallin' apple."

The men left to go back to their wagons but Willy stayed. He knew about some of the things Randolph had studied but one of them he had never heard of. "What's Latin?" he asked.

"We can talk about it tomorrow," Randolph said, "but an example would be that marking on your colt's forehead."

"That has to do with Latin?" Willy asked.

"Yes," was the Mountain Man's answer. "Latin is an ancient language the Romans used. The word 'circle' comes from the Latin word 'circus'."

"That's it." Willy shouted, jumping up and dancing a little jig beside the campfire.

"What's it?" Randolph puzzled.

"That's gotta be my horse's name. Circus. It's perfect!" Willy exclaimed.

Willy sat for a while after Randolph left to bed down and watched the fire die into glowing coals. He thought to himself, "The caravan, the strong man, the bearded lady, the clown, and now my colt is 'Circus'."

CHAPTER THREE

The first morning in Missouri, both James and Willy sat with Randolph at breakfast hoping to hear more of his tales before the wagon train struck out across the state.

Willy asked, "What's the biggest town we'll come to?"

"Well," Randolph answered, "the next one of any size we'll come to is Springfield but the biggest one is north of us on both the Illinois and Missouri sides of the river."

"Saint Louis?" said James.

"No." said the Mountain with a smile that puzzled the boys. "Cahokia."

James, brassy and good with geography said, "There's no such place."

"If we had time we could ride north and I'd show you." Randolph responded. "I learned about it from my mother. The Cherokees knew about it for hundreds of years. It's believed that over ten thousand Indians lived at the main site, which was as big as five miles long and five miles wide. Beyond that there could have been as many as twenty to thirty thousand living in surrounding settlements that ranged out fifty miles or more in every direction. There were thousands of pole and thatch houses, and many temples and public buildings."

"Indian legends," James said dismissively.

Ignoring the disdain Randolph continued, "And most impressive of all, there were as many as two hundred pyramids."

This was too much for James who rolled his eyes at Willy and turning back, said to Randolph with a chuckle, 'Pyramids, like in Egypt?"

"Different." he answered, "Made of terraced earth. The biggest, in the center of a large plaza, was said to be three terraces high. Towered well over a hundred feet with a palace on top. An account of a great happening that inspired the ancient peoples to build the city was passed down through centuries by the Cherokee fathers. They told of a brilliant ball of light in the sky near the Moon. It was several times as bright as Venus and lasted day and night for nearly a month."

Randolph now was ready to take up James' skepticism. "As a boy I had heard many stories from the Cherokee elders and that one was very hard to believe, but soon after I escaped England and made my way back to the wilds of America, I met an explorer named Henry Brackenridge. He had been to the Cahokia site and studied the place for weeks. His description matched up pretty well with what I learned as a boy. He was so astounded by his discovery that he wrote President Jefferson about it."

Willy was awestruck by the tale and silently vowed that someday he would go there and see for himself. James was wavering.

The Mountain Man, with a chunk of biscuit, wiped the remains of his breakfast from his tin pan, went to his horse and took something out of his saddle bag. He sat down with the boys and handed the object to Willy as a reward for his belief. It was a stone disk, larger in diameter than a biscuit but smaller than a pancake and thicker.

"Brackenridge," he said, "gave me three of these stones. He found many of them at the Cahokia site. It's called a 'chunkey' and was used in a game for hundreds of years by many Indian tribes. Another day I'll tell you how the game was played."

James was jealous of the gift but quietly pleased that he had learned about Cahokia. Randolph was at one moment a wild and wooly trapper, but at another moment he was what James imagined college professors were like.

As the wagon train moved across southern Missouri at its oxen pace, the rolling hills grew progressively steeper. Elijah fretted about the wear and tear on wagon brake shoes. James had been appointed official "brakeman" of the whole wagon train. Every morning he carried out his assignment to check the brake shoes on each wagon, pointing out any that needed to be replaced.

The morning of the third day across Missouri James found the shoes on Jesse Terry's wagon were badly worn and pointed it out to Jesse. He had been watching them closely for several days. Jesse, however, had a mind of his own and was not inclined to be taught anything by a wet-behind-the-ears teenager.

"Not to worry, Jimmy boy," Jesse said, "They're good for two or three more days." He had said much the same two days earlier just after the Mississippi crossing. Faithful to the assignment his father gave him, James decided to keep a close eye on the Terry wagon. Its most precious cargo was his sister Mary Ann. It was reassuring to him that Randolph was that day riding at the end of the wagon train beside Jesse's wagon. Into the afternoon each hill seemed steeper than the one before it and in some places there were frightening drop-offs on one side or the other of the trail. At what seemed the steepest down slope to that point, Elijah had the wagons roll down slowly one by one, each clearing the bottom and moving forward before the next one started down. Jesse's was the last in line.

Cresting the ridge and having gone no more than twenty yards with Jesse's hand firmly on the brake lever and Mary Ann sitting nervously beside him, there was a creaking sound. The wagon lurched forward a short distance, then a cracking sound and it picked up speed. Randolph realized what was happening. He jumped down from his horse and pulled Mary Ann down from the wagon. Jesse's two big mules began to lose their footing as the wagon pushed them forward. Pulling on the reins was futile. Jesse jumped to safety and stood watching as the wagon rolled ever faster and plunged over the side of the trail down a steep ravine. The sound from the mules was horrifying as they tumbled over and over with the wagon and crashed at the bottom. They lay beneath a pile of the shattered wagon, broken wheels and all the trunks and boxes of Jesse and Mary Ann's possessions. The canvas that once covered the wagon bows now lay draped over the wreckage like a funeral shroud. Elijah had watched in horror from below and rode quickly to the top where he, Randolph, Jesse and James made their way down through the rocky drop-off. The mules had to be shot and it took the whole afternoon for a chain line of Webb men to bring back up what could be salvaged. Most of their clothes survived but all their table settings and furniture was destroyed. One unbroken wagon wheel was rolled back up to the top. It was a time to help Jesse not berate him. No one needed to tell him he was a careless fool.

By the time what remained of the contents of the Terry wagon had been distributed through the other wagons in the train and the rest was tied on the sides, no daylight remained for moving on. Gathered for the evening meal, no one could think of anything much to say. Willy tried to cheer the family up by announcing that he had a name for his colt. "From today on his name is Circus," he said.

Willy explained what he had learned from Randolph about it being originally a Latin word that meant circle, but didn't fill out the other details of his carnival analogy. Peter might have liked being seen as the strong man and James would probably have been pleased with the role of clown, but there would have been no polite way to explain about the bearded lady.

Randolph was quick to discern what Willy was trying to do and morphed into his Swims Swift Water identity. He whispered to Willy, "Bring your colt to me," and said to the gathered Webb clan, "It was my grandfather, the Cherokee medicine man's responsibility to call down the Spirits who turned young colts into horses fit for a Cherokee brave. He passed on to me the medicine for that." Then he pulled a pouch of powder from the pocket of his deer skin coat, mixed part of it into some of the bacon grease left from the night's cooking, and threw the rest into the fire where it exploded with a green flash. He then faced Willy and the Colt with the spiritual ointment in his hand. After a long pause drew the attention of all the Webb men, women and children, he dipped his forefinger into the ointment, bowed his head and chanted something in Cherokee, then put a small drop of ointment right in the center of the white circle on the black colt's forehead. After another short chanted phrase, he rubbed the rest of the ointment from the colt's shoulder down to his flank. A wave of shivers along the colt's skin followed his hand.

Swims Swift Waters then turned to Willy, paused again to be sure everyone was still with him, and, placing one hand on each of Willy's shoulders said, "Circus is his name. He will grow to be a great stallion. Treat him well. Someday he will save your life."

Family members gathered in twos and threes afterward, offering each other their opinions about what they had witnessed. For Randolph young Willy's purpose had been served. Everyone's thoughts had been diverted from the unhappy events of the day and it would be left to Willy and Circus to make sense of the anointing and the prophecy.

The wagon train made good progress for the next ten days. Some of the hills were even steeper than where Jesse's wagon crashed, but his tragedy had convinced everyone to keep their brake shoes in tip top shape. Watching the landscape unfold, Willy wasn't inclined to describe what he saw as any kind of Paradise. Everywhere there were rocky outcroppings, not the kind of land one would want to drive a plow through.

Shortly before noon Randolph said they were approaching Springfield and a sprinkling of farms appeared along the trail. Each was plotted a good distance from its neighbors. Houses were laid out in two parts with a single roof covering both. Split rail fences surrounded each property angling back and forth. Many were sited near springs and streams. When Springfield appeared in the distance the wagon train stopped where other families were camping together in a large flat area. The first order of the day was to determine from each Webb wagon what supplies they wanted from town. Elijah took one of the buckboards, called for James and Willy to come along and help, and together they drove in to find the Trading Post.

Willy's task was to mind the horse and buckboard while his father and James went in to buy supplies. He was amazed by the parade of people that passed by. There were oddly dressed men wearing black coats and black broad brimmed hats, soldiers in uniform, trappers with their furs, but most interesting of all were the Indians. Three Indians in a line passed so close to the buckboard Willy could have reached out and touched them. They were carrying bunches of fox and beaver pelts. The first in line was as tall as any of the taller Webb men. The second, Willy judged, could have been half a foot taller than the first, and the third was the tallest man he had ever seen. Willy guessed seven foot. The head of each was shaved in the same way, leaving only a patch of hair no bigger than a man's hand and about two inches long. Out of the center of the patch a long braid hung down to their waists. There was something dyed red in the short hair that looked like a deer's tail. They wore silver bracelets, beads around their necks and small things hung from their ears. Each Indian was naked to the waist and short flaps of some sort of animal skin covered their privates, back and front. Bands covered by polished shells and beads were around their calves and on their feet were moccasins. No drawing that Willy had ever seen captured the reality of these giant colorful men.

Willy looked up to see his father and James coming out of the Trading Post. In Elijah's hand was something wrapped in a cloth, which he put in his pocket. James was pushing a hand truck piled up with supplies. Willy jumped down from the buckboard, ran to help them and before either of them could speak to him he blurted out, "I just saw the most amazin' thing. Three Indians even taller than Jabez. I reckon the tallest must have been seven foot."

"That tall! You don't say. Way taller than even Jabez? " Elijah smiled over at James. It was clear to Willy neither of them believed him and the Indians were nowhere in sight. On the ride back to their camp and as the supplies were distributed Willy said nothing more. He thought Randolph might know of such men but, fearing more disbelief, he kept what he had seen to himself and hoped that whatever tribe the Indians came from they were peaceful. There was no one to tell him they were Wa-Saw-See, otherwise known as Osage. There were no taller men than they anywhere in the country.

After supper and clearing up, Ben urged J.C. to get out his fiddle. His reluctance was not convincing, but shortly he gave in and people from the other wagon trains came over. He was not the best of fiddlers, but the children started to dance about and were followed by the young adults when he launched into a Virginia reel. An old man in a tattered hat from another family joined in with his fiddle. There was a sense of relief from the people of the Webb wagon train whose spirits were sagging from the long trip and their troubles along the way. The rising gaiety was infectious and soon the party was going strong. After about an hour when everyone was danced out, the men gathered around the Webb campfire. Pipes were packed and lit. From somewhere a jug of liquor appeared.

Ben, the second oldest of Elijah's sons, who had a very engaging personality, broke the ice. "I'm Ben Webb from Overton County, Tennessee. You folks all come from as far away?"

"Even farther. Massachusetts," said the older of two men, whose wagon was one of the last to roll in that evening. "We're going out to Kansas."

"Gonna farm wheat?" Ben asked.

"Not exactly," the second of the two men replied. The group waited for something further, but nothing more was volunteered and it left a bit of tension in the air.

Jesse introduced himself, picked up the conversation and, with his typical lack of concern that he might offend, said, "Kansas wouldn't be for me. We keep hearin' about the troubles out there and along the border with Mizzoury." Not waiting for any disagreement he added, "Lot of hell being raised. One side coming over to steal Mizzoury slaves and Mizzoury people takin' the fight back into Kansas. Houses and crops burned, cattle stole, tarrin' and featherin', even people bein' hacked up."

Jesse was gathering steam. "Guess y'all heard what happened just this past May. Place called Potawatamie Creek.

Crazy abolitionist man by the name of John Brown from up New York way with his sons and some other men. Attacked some Kansas farmers. Way I heard it, they dragged five men out of their cabins, knifed them, cut off their hands, and bludgeoned them to death with their families lookin' on. Didn't even take time to ask the men what their view was 'bout owin' Negras."

The older of the two Massachusetts men leaned forward but appeared to be giving careful consideration to a response. "And what position do you take, Mr. Terry, about one man owning another?" he said.

"Position?" Jesse blurted back. "I'll tell you what's true. People from one part of the country ain't got any right to tell people from other parts how to live their life, what's right and what's wrong. Man like John Brown come all self-righteous onto my farm with bloody intent is gonna meet up with some hot lead."

Ben, who often found himself the mediator between older and younger brothers, broke in hoping to soften Jesse's harsh comments, but grounded his contentions in the Good Book. He said to the two men, "Friends, you're askin' about our beliefs but not volunteering your own about the bloody deeds of a man like Brown. I'll tell you what I believe. I reckon you know the Bible story of Ham, the son of Noah and his sin of seein' his father naked. Ham's son Canaan and all his generations were cursed."

Ben, the best in the family in Good Book memorizing, continued, "It's all there in Genesis where it says, 'Cursed be Canaan; a servant of servants shall he be unto his brethren.' Any student of the Good Book knows that the meanin' of the name Ham is 'black.' Those that have black men as their slaves ain't the cause of their trouble. They done it to themselves way back in the beginnin' times."

Ben added, "By the way, friend, what was your name?"

"It's Daniel."

"Daniel what?"

"Daniel Sumner."

Ben's Bible quote, which for him was the final word, hung heavily in the air and Sumner left it there. All the makin's for a hot argument were there, but Sumner offered nothing more than a stern look. Fortunately, the mood shifted with the soft comment from a man sitting next to Sumner. "My people are Quakers and believe the Bible, but we think that the Declaration of Independence was on the right track when it pronounced that all men are equal. Above all we don't think any difference between the views that men hold is ever settled by violence."

The short silence that followed was broken by the sounds of women from the different families saying their good nights as they headed back to their wagons to bed the children down. It provided the men a timely excuse to end their discussion. Willy, who had been so totally engrossed that he had ignored the signals of his body, headed off into the woods for relief.

Returning to the Webb camp he passed by the wagon of the two Massachusetts men. He stopped in the dark when he heard voices coming from behind their wagon. Sumner's partner spoke, "Let's open a case and break out a couple of Beecher's Bibles. We could run into Bushwackers before we get across the line into Kansas. That Jesse guy sounded like one to me."

Willy crept closer and saw the men had dropped down the tail gate to their wagon and were lifting the lid of a long wooden crate, one of several filling their covered wagon. In the faint light of the lamp they had hung from the back top bow, Willy watched Sumner pull a rifle out of the straw in the crate. It looked new.

Back in the Webb camp, Willy crawled under his father's wagon and curled up in his bed roll. All the men in his family had rifles but these men from the East had a wagon full. His sleep was fitful. He dreamed that a line of men shouldering their rifles were firing at each other point blank, then they all turned toward him and simultaneously fired. When he woke the next morning he was reluctant to admit that he had been snooping, but decided that he should tell his father what he had seen. Willy's tales tended to be long and full of more details than were needed, but Elijah listened patiently and then responded, "I've heard of a churchman name of Beecher back East who raises money for guns for the Kansas people who oppose slavery. His critics call the guns "Beecher's Bibles." Then after a thoughtful moment he added, "Let's keep this quiet, Willy. Our trail today will take us on a different route from these men. We've already had our share of trouble and don't need any more."

Willy was pleased to share an important secret with his father. It made him feel like a man. He had to bite his tongue not to tell Randolph as he started another day up on the wagon seat beside him. Willy liked to think of it as "ridin' shotgun." What he did decide to break silence about was the tall Indians he had seen in Springfield. It came as no surprise to Randolph who said, "They're Osage, Willy. Their Indian name is 'Wa-Saw-See' and many are tall like the ones you saw. They're fierce warriors and proud people. They've ranged for generations over the land we're rolling through, all the way north and south from the Missouri River to the Arkansas River and from the Mississippi to Kansas, east to west. From way back in history there weren't any white men in all that territory. The Osage Chiefs, however, failed their people; they signed treaties that gave away all their land. Now their numbers are shrinking and they've been pushed west of the Missouri-Kansas border. The only time one sees them much these days is when a few come east to trade."

It was a warm October morning, what Willy heard some people call "Indian Summer." His father had told everyone that morning that the last leg of the trip would now take only two days, three at the most. Willy hoped that leg would be trouble free. Everyone needed all their energies. The big challenge would be to build shelter for all the families as quickly as they could. October would soon turn into November. Winter was less than a few weeks away.

Willy was still full of questions for the Mountain Man and hoped to ride shotgun with him again, but at breakfast he was nowhere to be seen. Willy couldn't believe that he would leave without saying a word. Apparently he had gotten up before anyone else that morning, saddled up his pinto and left with his donkey in tow. For the first two hours out on the trail Willy kept thinking he might have just gone off to shoot some game or something, but by the time the caravan stopped at noon, it was clear he was gone. Several times during the day Willy took out his Mountain Man treasure, the chunkie. Randolph viewed such things as magical and Willy thought, maybe someday its power would cause their paths to cross again.

J.C. , who had come up to Missouri earlier and purchased land anticipating the family's move up from Tennessee, moved his wagon into the lead position. To Willy the countryside on to the southwest corner of Missouri was much the same as the rocky land the caravan passed through approaching Springfield from the east. Little he had seen yet looked like promising farm land, let alone any kind of 'promised land.' His Mother, uncertain from the get-go about the wisdom of leaving Tennessee, had voiced her doubts a number of times during the journey. The family's decision turned heavily on J.C.'s enthusiasm but his mother knew him better than anyone else and she had doubts about his judgment.

In the late afternoon of the second day on the last leg of the long journey the wagon train pulled into a village called Sarcoxie. An old man running the grist mill there was full of tales about the area. He said the mill was set up there on Center Creek twenty some odd years earlier by a man named Thacker Vivion. By all accounts, the old man said, he was the first white man in the area. Came over from Kentucky where he was born. A blacksmith shop had been there earlier and Vivion added a saw mill.

"Thacker," the old mill man said, "was an adventurous sort of man, restless. Said as a young man he fought in the War of 1812. When he came here it was Indian land."

"Sarcoxie," the old man continued, "was the name of the local Indian chief. Meant 'Rising Sun.' Wasn't long before Thacker got the travel itch. Headed off down to Texas on some adventure a few years back. His son and grandchildren live a ways west from here."

In the old man's rambling the name of the man who set up the mill caught Willy's attention. It was the first and middle name of one of his young cousins, Thacker Vivion Webb–a mystery to be explored.

There was great excitement in the camp the next morning when the wagon train rolled out. Elijah had said that, barring the unexpected, they would reach the end of their journey, Jasper County, before sundown. Driving the animals harder than was wise, they arrived in the late afternoon at the farm of Elijah's brother, James Crittendon Webb.

Elijah insisted that two wagons be unloaded as quickly as possible so he could haul everyone over to a spot near Turkey Creek to see the sprawl of land J.C. had bought for him the previous year. It lay not far northwest of where James and his wife Clarissa had built their cabin a year earlier. Dusk was creeping in by the time the wagons stopped at the top of a low hill, so it was not easy to see what the land looked like. For months Elijah had been studying J.C.'s rough sketch of the land's features, trying to decide what the best spot was for a cabin. He pointed down the slope toward a flat area beside a large oak tree and said to the Webb clan members standing around him, "That's where we'll build our new home. Gotta get right at it tomorrow morning if we hope to beat the winter."

Willy saw his mother, standing beside his father, lean in to whisper something in his ear. He couldn't hear what she said but he did catch his father's reply, "Overton County ain't home anymore, Martha Jane."

A nip in the air the next morning and a light frost on the ground sharpened the sense of urgency that everyone felt. Cabins for each couple and their children, along with one or two common barns and some sheds, would be built one by one by the whole clan working together. Some of the cabins would be built on adjacent lots. Two were more than a mile farther north.

In Tennessee Willy's only use of an axe was chopping firewood. To bring down a small tree took a few days practice and some tips from old Peter before he learned how to strike the same spot with several blows. He also learned to use the full length of the axe handle to get the most power from his swing. Notching out logs for the corner joints called for the most skill and was dangerous, standing on the log and cutting the "V" between your boots. That was left to the adults.

Without the Webb's slaves the rush to beat the oncoming winter would not have been possible. Negroes and whites worked side by side, but the slaves usually drew the harder jobs. Willy noticed that when slaves worked together, such as Peter and young Jack cutting down a big tree, one on each side, they created a vocal rhythm to pace their work. It seemed they got more accomplished with less effort. Their cabins, however, would be last ones finished and were much cruder.

Priority had been given to building Elijah's cabin, which would be the finest of the lot. The logs cut for it were mostly oak and walnut. A few were maple. Careful attention was given to the chinking between the logs. It was an exotic mixture of grasses, clay, sand, animal hair and anything else that would bind the mixture. The two ceiling joists were elm. A choice walnut tree provided the door. Many of the other cabins would start out with dirt floors, but the time was taken to hand-hew one inch planks for Elijah's floor. Stones were brought up from a nearby creek for the chimney and hearth.

It would be the largest cabin by far, measuring a little more than eighteen by thirty-four feet. Elijah, Martha Jane and the five children still living with them, who slept in lofts, had twice as much room as any of the other families.

So many trees had been felled that Willy could imagine an open field to plow. The stumps, Ben told him were the hardest part. Even with the strongest team of mules, it was hard going. The biggest sometimes had to be blasted out. At the head of the swath of tree stumps was Elijah's barn. Apart from the slave cabins, it was the last structure to go up.

Work done for the day, Elijah with Willy beside him, washed up in a newly carved out log water trough. Willy sat down on a large stump looking to the west and warmed himself in what remained of the afternoon sun. His father had gone over to the family's wagon and came back with an object wrapped in burlap. Willy slid over to make room for his father and said, "The barn's gonna be a great place this winter for Circus."

"It's his barn and also as much yours as mine, son," Elijah replied. "You've worked as hard as any of the grown men these weeks. I can tell you've learned a lot and I see muscle on you that wasn't there back in Tennessee. Men do a lot of different chores in life, Willy. They chop down trees, take care of their animals, plow their fields, and tend to all the other things needed by their families. But a man isn't complete if he fails to do special things for himself, things for his own mind and heart."

Willy's mother, especially when reading the Bible to the children, often spoke of what she called, "The things of the Spirit," but his father rarely did. "Learn to appreciate the finer things in life," Elijah continued, "the things that inspire. Schoolin's important. You must learn not only to read well, but to understand what you read. As much as you can, learn what great men have thought and done. And then there's music. A man must love music, not just to hear it, but to make it."

Elijah unfolded the burlap to reveal a violin case. "I had Ben pick this up for me when we were at the trading post in Springfield," he said, "My father gave one to me when the family was still living in Virginia. And he taught me how to play."

Willy opened the case and took out the violin. Being left handed like his father, he took it by the neck with his right hand and put it under his chin as he had seen his father do. "I'd bet good money that you'll be a fine fiddler one day, Willy. And if you're as lucky as me to have fine sons, I'll expect you to teach them how to fiddle and play together with them."

Even though choked up, Willy somehow got out the words, "Thank you, father," but the real gratitude was what Elijah saw in his son's eyes. If he had tried to imagine what more was going through Willy's mind, his guess would not have been far off. Willy was silently vowing that he would be the best fiddler he could be, might even be better than J.C. Good enough to play alongside his father.

Willy was huddled under his quilt, hiding from the coldest so far of the early winter mornings when James woke him. "Get yourself up, Willy," he said, "you're gonna have to pick up my chores this morning."

"Your chores?" Willy mumbled in objection.

"Yeh, my chores. Father says I have to go out with him and lay out a cemetery."

That got Willy to peek out from under the quilt. "Cemetery?" he said, "This time of year? Who died?"

"Nobody, far's I know," James replied. But father, and I don't know who else, got the idea in their heads and I know better'n to ask a lot of questions. Still, I'm wonderin' if they might be worried about Mary Ann."

For Willy it wasn't enough to just wonder. As soon as he had finished James' morning chores he went to his mother who explained that Mary Ann had gotten worse since they arrived in Missouri. She explained, "What we gotta do is pray for her to get stronger and let God do the rest. But people get old and die, Willy, and your father thought it was wise to set aside land for a cemetery now. We've already got a name for it, 'Harmony Grove,' and there's also gonna be room for a church there someday."

Less than three weeks had passed before the cemetery was needed but it wasn't for Mary Ann.

Ruthie, J.C's wife, was pregnant on the trip up from Tennessee but she lost the baby, a daughter.

Willy's mother said she was "stillborn"—didn't come into the world alive. Old Peter made a rough hewn little coffin for the body. One by one everyone in the family, except Mary Ann, passed by the little grave and dropped in a handful of dirt. Above the women's sobs Willy heard Mary Ann coughing. She stood back from the rest of the family, thinner than when they reached Missouri and there was a darkness around her eyes. Jesse was supporting her with his hand around her waist. Jane, Ben's wife, was on the other side holding her hand, but most of the other family members shied away from her. When Willy asked his mother why, she explained that the doctor believed Mary Ann had consumption. "Everyone knows it can be passed from one person to another," she explained. Willy began to think that he might catch it if he got too close to his sister and was embarrassed by his fear.

Less than two weeks had passed when the second grave was dug at New Harmony. On a windy December day the family passed closer to Mary Ann, now not fearful, but grieving. Willy had a number of questions whirling in his mind, all of which began with the word "why," but he kept them to himself. It was only in the every night reading of the Bible that he found any consolation. Mary Ann had been his favorite sister.

It was a nightly ritual for the children to gather round their mother to hear her read from the Good Book. She often said the way to read the Bible was to begin at the beginning, and her progress from the early days of the journey up from Tennessee until then had brought her to the Book of Job. Willy, who in the past hadn't always listened closely, didn't remember much about that story from readings in past years. Now, sitting with the others near the hearth at his mother's feet, it caught his attention.

There seemed no end to the horrors that Job experienced when God tested him—how fire came down from Heaven and burnt up all his cattle and servants, how a great wind killed his sons. And on top of that God even spread boils over Job's whole body. Willy understood that some of the tales in the Bible were tales about real people and events. Others he understood to be more like fairy tales, whose purpose was to teach some lesson. Which the Story of Job was he was not sure and it was not the kind of question his mother liked to hear. If he was a real man, Willy found it beyond understanding that God, who was supposed to be a loving father, would test one of his faithful children so fiercely. The only explanation his mother offered was that it teaches us to face up to whatever bad things came our way with determination, courage and faith. She added a saying which he had heard from her on many other occasions, "What don't kill you only makes you stronger."

For weeks Willy expected Mary Ann in her lively good spirits to come bursting through their cabin door, excited about some new bird song she had heard or some wild flower she had found. His best diversion from grief was trying to play his new fiddle. James and Eli laughed at the screeching sounds Willy made, covered their ears and left the room. The new coon dogs his father had bought to replace the ones he had to leave in Tennessee howled from out in their pen. Usually he took his practice out to the barn, where he sat in the straw in Circus' stall. If anyone would lend him a sympathetic ear, surely it would be his horse and by and large, the growing colt seemed not to mind. Only now and then would he flinch at a piercing note and lay his ears back.

Elijah's faith in Willy's potential was well placed. Week by week he and his fiddle became better friends and at the same time his sad thoughts about Mary Ann diminished. It was only three months after the family's second trip to Harmony Grove that Elijah, who had been inconspicuously checking on his son's progress, called Willy over to where he was sitting in his favorite chair, lighting up his pipe. It was his every-night-after-dinner routine. The children called it his "announcement chair." From time to time he called the

family around him, or in some instances just one of his children, and spoke of something important. He said to Willy,
"I trust you're goin' to the barn dance tomorrow night," and
not waiting for the answer he added, "'Bring your fiddle with
you. I want you to play with me and J.C." There was no room
for Willy to see it as a question or to object. All through the
next day he fretted and each time he tried to practice it went
badly, but once the first tune was struck up at the barn dance
he played well and proudly. Any failing his friends and family
might have noticed he made up for by now and then dancin'
a little jig while he played. He was better than he realized.

Circus, who had been the patient audience as Willy
learned his instrument, now had his own learnin' to do. It
was time for him to meet the bridle and saddle. Willy had
never liked the expression "breakin' a horse". Something in
him was offended by the cruelty it implied. Circus was his
friend and Willy thought they could meet the challenge
without either of them getting hurt. He decided not to just
throw on a saddle, climb up on him and hang on until Circus'
spirit was broken. James his brother who clearly thought that
Willy was just afraid of being thrown off and bustin' his butt
said, "So how you gonna do it?"

"I got my ideas," Willy answered.

He also ignored J.C.'s offer, "Give'm to me for a day,
Willy boy, and I'll show him who's boss." Circus was now
a powerful stallion and Willy would have enjoyed seeing
him turn J.C. into a clown, but this was his horse and he
had his plan.

On the first day he put a long rope on Circus and,
standing in the center of the corral, he ran him around the

perimeter, first clockwise then the reverse. On the first few trips around Circus tossed his head, snorted, and from time to time kicked up his hind legs but then, after a few trips back and forth around he relaxed into a smooth gait and seemed to enjoy the exercise.

After three days of that when Willy added the saddle there was only a flinch, a snort, and a small side step. After a half hour of the same circling with Willy holding the long rope, he unhooked the rope and walked away ignoring Circus. In a few steps he felt a strong nudge in the center of his back. Circus had followed him and wanted more attention. The next step, getting up in the saddle, was easier than Willy had expected. In short order horse and rider were making the same circles together and Willy was teaching his big black stallion what it meant when he laid the reins to one side of his neck or the other. They had bonded on the first day back in Tennessee when Willy picked him out. Now the two moved gracefully together like one.

Willy had been so absorbed with his fiddle and his horsemanship that he hadn't paid much attention to the tales of gangs of men riding around the country at night raising hell until, on an early Spring morning in 1859, Elijah's brother James burst in on their breakfast.

"Big trouble last night," he exclaimed. "Mrs. Keenan from over cross Turkey Creek came poundin' at my door. She was shakin' and weepin,' barefoot and wearin' a night gown soaked down the front in blood. When Clarissa and I got her calmed down a bit she said a half dozen men rode up to their house late at night. When her husband, Henry, went out to see what they wanted, they shot him down in cold blood."

"Oh, dear God," Willy's mother cried out. Elijah just shook his head slowly. Willy and the other children didn't know what to say, but he remembered the Mountain Man's warning that angry white men on both sides of the Missouri-Kansas border were more of a danger than Indians.

Following the admonition that one shouldn't speak ill of the dead, neither Elijah nor his brother James would have said anything about how much most of Keenan's neighbors disliked him. He had a second farm northwest over near Elijah's friend Jonathan Rusk's land where he had set up a tenant farmer. Both the tenant and his wife had come down with serious illnesses. Some of their neighbors feared that they both might die. Four of Keenan's own farmhands, who had learned of the tenant couple's troubles, complained to him that the tenant was not keeping up with his work. Without realizing that each of his own workers had coveted the tenant arrangement for himself, without telling the tenant what the specific criticisms of him were or giving him a chance to defend himself, Keenan, a short little man with a nasty temper, blew his top. That same night he rode over to the tenant's place and told them to pack up and leave.

Jonathan, who told the story to Elijah earlier that year, had said, "In my experience it's often the short little men who cause the world a lot of its problems." He added, "When the Lord gave out common sense and common decency he skipped over Keenan." Jonathan didn't have to explain to Elijah that short stature was a problem in his own family. Of the five older Rusk sons, David, who was much shorter than all of his tall brothers, gave him the most grief. And Jonathan didn't use the title by which a number of men in the county referred to Keenan, "Little Fart." Both men had also heard of the tenant's reaction, but didn't call it up out of sympathy for Keenan's widow. It was no secret in the county that the tenant, Jeremiah Rutledge, a tall determined man, had voiced a solemn oath, "I'm gonna nurse my wife back to health, scare the Grim Reaper away from us both, and one day I'll piss on Keenan's grave."

Martha Jane left Elijah and their children to clear up after breakfast and went back with James to his house to take Mrs. Keenan home and help her with arrangements for burying her husband. Elijah went out to the barn to muck out the horse stalls and Willy went along to help. After an hour of what to Willy was the one unpleasant thing about owning a horse, he and his father went out to the well for a drink. Elijah hauled up a bucket, dipped the tin cup in and handed it to Willy, then dipped one for himself.

Father and son sat quietly together, both still shaken by the morning's news. Elijah said, "Someday, Willy, you and your brothers may have to help me defend the family and what's ours. You'll hear men like last night's riders called 'Jayhawkers.' The worst of them would as soon shoot a man as look at him. You're a pretty good shot with a squirrel rifle, Willy, but it's something else to point a gun at a man and fire. I've never had a man shoot at me and I've never shot a man, but we gotta be ready. I fear times are gonna get a lot worse."

All the Webb men, fathers and older sons, and sons-in-law gathered that night in Elijah's cabin. His anger boiling over, Jesse was the first to speak. The views he expressed when he tangled with the abolitionists at Springfield had grown even stronger after the family arrived at their new Missouri homes and the attack on the Keenans pushed him over the edge. "It's more of the violence that crazy old man, John Brown, started over in Kansas before we got here. Whether we like it or not, the fat's now in the fire. None of our families can feel safe."

Ben, who was less volatile, carried the thought further. "We have to appreciate that the Webbs and our kin are big targets. We own as many Negras as any family in the County. More than most. These people from across the state line believe they're on a mission from God. I've heard that one of their leaders, who claims to be a pacifist, says he'd never harm any man made in the image of God, but in his readin' of the Bible we southern slave owners are 'beasts from Hell.' Killin' folks like us is their duty. They can do it in good conscience."

Jesse jumped back in, "They ain't got no right to tell us how to live, what property we can own or what to do with it." He didn't notice Elijah, his father-in-law, scowl at his swearing when he added, "The self-righteous bastards. I've heard some pretty bad things about them—that what the Negra-lovin' northerners really got on their mind is not set-ting slaves free. They wanna get the slave women in their beds. Well, I ain't got no women slaves, but I'll shoot any abo-litionist that dares step on my land."

Elijah stood up walked over to the hearth and knocked the ashes out of his pipe. Everyone waited for him to speak. He didn't comment on Jesse's last point about slave women, but speaking softly to calm emotions in the room said, "We'll pray than no one here has to shoot anyone. Don't forget what the Good Book says, 'The man that lives by the sword dies by the sword.' These bad times will pass. God willin', all of us and our children will live to see better days. We won't lose our faith and we won't become beasts. We'll pray together like everythin' depends on God, but we'll keep our rifles ready and our powder dry, like everythin' depends on us."

Despite the family's worst fears and sporadic conflict back and forth across the border, the next few months were ones of steady progress. Next to the cemetery a church was built. Both were called "Harmony Grove." Willy, who was having a growth spurt, was showing more muscle and kept pace with the older men clearing land for pasture and crops. To the family's Negroes fell much of the heavy work. Without them, all that was done would have taken much longer. They worked as hard as the oxen, Willy judged, and they had no more to say than the animals. The oxen only worked when their yokes were put on, but the Webb Negras never dropped their yokes, invisible yokes.

Late that September invisible forces of another kind struck the family. It began with Willy's sister, Anneliza, who was two years older than he. Willy could see that when she complained for several days of headaches and had trouble sleeping, their mother became very concerned. She was always quick to look at tongues, down irritated throats and check foreheads for temperature, especially if anyone looked flushed. When she felt Annie's forehead, she said, "Oh, sweetie, you're hot as a clothes iron." Willy thought his mother also looked a bit flushed.

One after another the family fell ill. In a few days Annie had broken out in reddish spots and her fever didn't break. Willy was the next to fall. First, it was just feeling so out of sorts that he had to pass his chores to James. Then his belly began to swell up. He had unrelenting bellyaches and what his father called "the runs." In two days spots like Annie's appeared on his back. His heart pounded in his chest like a runaway horse and his mouth was as dry as cotton. Their house Negras helped James and Juliette, his sister seven years older than he, care for him and Annie, but as the days passed Willy felt he was falling into some kind of nightmare world and couldn't find his way out. He had a sense that Eli was lying sick in a bed beside him. Things swirled around him—cool cloths for his head, water to sip, slop jars and figures that grew ever more ghostly. He couldn't tell what was a dream and what was real. Soon the figures all morphed into angels. A host of them gathered around him and one, larger than all the others, with large wings, was surrounded by a white glow. Leaning down to him, she took his hand and whispered, "Come with me, Willy, come with me."

CHAPTER FOUR

Willy could hear voices rising up to him in the loft. As his head began slowly to clear, it was the sound of someone crying. It was Juliette whose sobbing always came up from so deep in her soul that it touched Willy. Bit by bit he constructed the world around him–Eli lying on a bed next to him breathing heavily, the top of the ladder rising up to the loft from below, his eyes adjusting to the faint light from below, the long sleeping gown he wore damp with sweat. He turned to the side of his bed, swung his feet to the floor and, holding on to the bedpost to steady himself, he stood up, hardly able to support his own weight. With his right hand sliding along the loft wall to steady himself, he made his way to the edge of the loft and looked down. The room below was dim, the only light came from the hearth and several candles placed around the room.

Holding tight to the ladder he made his way down slowly, each rung a challenge.

Juliette was sitting in her mother's rocking chair sobbing as she rocked back and forth. When she saw Willy she jumped up, ran to him and threw her arms around him, still sobbing, "Oh Willy, Willy." Looking behind her, his eyes adjusted to the soft light which was steady from the candles but flickering from the hearth. He understood why she was crying. On the family's large trestle table, which Willy's father had made, and a second table that must have come from another Webb home, lay two full sized coffins. Juliette collected herself long enough to say, "We've lost them, Willy. We've lost them both." He knew instantly who had died.

The "nervous fever," dreaded by all their neighbors, had swept through the family, taking Elijah and Martha Jane, Willy's parents, but sparing him and Eli. Since there were only two coffins, he hoped Anneliza had also survived. One by one the older children, who had done everything they could to help their parents survive, returned from supper at their homes to their parents' cabin. There was a lot of "Praise God," as each in turn hugged Willy.

From outside the cabin a mournful sound of voices wafted in. It was their slaves who had come to pay their respects. Singing from deep within their own experience, their voices blended as if they were a practiced choir. Willy picked out the rich soulful baritone of Old Peter:

"I am a poor wayfarin' stranger, while passin' through this world below. There is no sickness toil nor danger in that bright land to which I go. I'm goin' there to meet my Father. He said he'd meet me when I come. I'm just goin' over Jordan. I'm just goin' over home."

As they sang outsized fleecy flakes of snow fell on their heads and shoulders. It was only the end of October and the trees were still dressed in their foliage.

Had there not been such great sadness, the next morning would have been glorious. The sun lit up the red and yellow leaves and the snow that was sprinkled on them brightly answered back. It was a morning to walk through the woods and drink in the mix of colors, but the family had gathered to discuss burial plans. From the new preacher at Harmony Grove church, the most educated man in their part of the county, they learned that the malady that had struck their home was called "Typhoid." He explained that no one knew for sure where it came from or how one caught it, but he warned that it could spread quickly, could come back and kill those who weren't stricken the first time around. He urged the family to cremate the bodies as a precaution. Everyone objected, but it was agreed that they should be put in the ground promptly. One speculation was that the disease could have been caused by some corruption seeping into Elijah's well. J.C. and Ben laid plans to seal it up that day.

The reach of months into 1860 was a time for slowly coming to grips with the death of Elijah and Martha Jane. Their older children, Paulina, J.C., and Ben were drawn back to a more normal life by the demands of their own families. It was not as easy for Willy, James, Eli and their sisters. It fell to them to take over the family farm. James was named "Head of Household" by Elijah's will, which made him responsible for his siblings and the slaves that went with the farm.

The will's distribution of the Webb slaves was convo-
luted. To Paulina went Lucy, who was about fifty. J.C. got
Jack, twenty, and Sarah about twelve. Ben drew Old Peter,
who thought he was about fifty, and Sam, thirteen. As
guardian for his younger brother James, Ben received
Caroll, who was listed as forty, and Jean, about eight. Ben
who was guardian also for Anneliza, took charge of the
beautiful light-skinned thirty year old Julia and her ten-year-
old daughter, Harriet. John, seven, was left to Willy, but Ben
was also guardian for him. It seemed rather like a joke that
Willy's little brother Eli, who was only thirteen, would
receive six year old Granville. He was Julia's child and the
lightest of all the Negro boys. Eli was also on Ben's guardian
list. Various sums of money went out to some from the
estate and others paid sums back to it for the slaves that
passed to them as guardians. All in all, by the time Elijah,
died he held fourteen slaves: three adult men, three adult
women, three boys teenage or younger, and five girls
teenage or younger.

By the next year new arrangements were made for the
slaves, putting thirteen under the supervision of James, who
was now fully responsible for his father's farm with Willy, Eli
and the girls helping. Willy, still grieving for his parents, began
slowly to recover his strength. At first each time he stood up
quickly the room spun around him and sometimes the edges
of his vision grew dark. James tried to help by assigning light
chores at first. Willy had objected to his first assignment, collecting eggs. That was "women's work." But he quickly grad-
uated to more manly things, work in the barn. To make that
move official James had touched Willy on first one shoulder
and then the other with a short horse whip and pronounced

him "Prince of Horse Muck." With each pitchfork full of staw and horse manure Willy grew stronger.

More to Willy's liking was exercising Circus. A time or two at first when, woozy spells hit, he had to grab the saddle horn to keep from falling off. Circus had reached his full growth–sixteen hands, shiny black coat covering powerful muscles. Galloping across their meadow the two moved as one, but Circus sometimes had a mind of his own. At close to full speed they approached the steepest hill on the Webb farm, a rocky outcropping. Just as Willy was about to lay the reins on his neck to turn right at the base of the hill, Circus made his own decision. He dropped his head slightly into the gallop and charged straight up the hill, throwing rocks and gravel down behind him. Willy was both frightened and thrilled. When they reached the top he drew in a deep breath and turned to look back down the rocky incline. It was an adventure Willy would keep to himself.

Three days after his fifteenth birthday Willy Webb and his older brother James were working with two of their slaves, old Peter and young Jack, grubbing up tree stumps west of the Webb cabin, when they heard what first sounded like a clap of thunder. It seemed odd. The morning sky was clear. Several more rumbles followed in quick succession, then other explosions that sounded a bit different. The two sounds mixed together and kept repeating. James looked at Willy and said what they both were thinking, "That's gotta be cannon fire!" Neither of them noticed the look that passed between their slave men and did not hear what Old Peter said to Jack, thirty years his junior. Peter's strategy for survival and sustaining hope was humor, and there was a twinkle in his eye when he put his axe head on the ground, cupped his hands to lean on the handle and said softly to Jack, "Sounds to me more like the 'Sweet chariot' swingin' low, comin' from over 'cross Jordan comin' fer to carry us home." Young Jack smiled and nodded, but was not totally certain what Peter meant.

The noise thudded against all four sweaty chests, two black and two white, and echoed off the house and barn. It seemed to be coming from the northeast over Carthage way. It couldn't have been Jayhawkers or Bushwhackers, who rode light and carried only pistols and rifles. Something even more serious than their rampaging was happening. Willy was ready to saddle up Circus, grab his father's shotgun and go see what the ruckus was, but James objected, "Hold up, Willy. We better try to find what it's all about before we ride into a pack of trouble."

Through the afternoon rumors passed from farm to farm. Some had heard that several hundred Union men from up north were chasing Governor Jackson's State Guard south after a clash at Boonville. Others said it was a thousand or more Yankees, but that Jackson's recruits numbered as many as six times that and that they had stood their ground north of Carthage between Dry Fork and Possum Creek. Most everyone round about knew that Jackson's cavalry had few weapons and his infantry, as many as two thousand, had only the squirrel rifles and shotguns they brought with them from their farms. Others had no weapons at all.

"There may be a whole lot more of them than the Federals," James said, "but they're a rag tag bunch and know damned little about bein' soldiers." He thought the locals couldn't have had much of a chance. Just as the summer sun was getting low in the sky, a neighbor, Wes Rusk, rode up to the Webb cabin on his way back home from Carthage. William Wesley Rusk was the second oldest of six brothers, the sons of a prominent landowner, Jonathan Rusk. The Rusks, a good hard working clan, had come to the county from Indiana nearly twenty years earlier and were well established before the Webb clan arrived from Tennessee. They were among the first Jasper County farmers the Webbs met when they arrived in 1856.

Wes, who was ten years or so older than James, stopped to water his horse and take a break from the saddle, but clearly was eager to get on home. On ordinary days, when he rode by their farm, he often stopped for a friendly chat and early on Willy noticed that, despite their age difference, Wes never treated him like a child. Dipping into the bucket at their well for a drink, he confirmed some of what they had gathered through the day. He reckoned that dozens or more had died on each side with a lot more wounded. He had seen some men blown apart by artillery.

Eager to get on back home, Wes swung up into the saddle. He barely had both feet in the stirrups when his horse spun around toward the west, knowing its own way home. Wes knew that the southern sentiments of the Webb clan reached back several generations, and the Webb boys knew that, while the Rusks were not belligerent folks, they sympathized with the Northern cause.

Tipping his hat in friendly recognition of the Negroes who kept several yards back from the conversation, he exclaimed to the Webb brothers, "Looks like it's all out war now! I hope we won't be shootin' at each other!" He had said it light-heartedly, almost mindlessly, but as he put his spurs to his horse's flanks his comments quickly turned sad, then alarming. The thought came to mind that he should go back and say something to make sure they didn't see it as a hostile comment, but knew instinctively that in such matters more talk usually clouded things up further.

West of the Webb farm in the direction of the Kansas border, on a stretch of prairie between Center Creek on the north and Turkey Creek on the south, were a number of land plots owned by Jonathan Rusk and his sons. When Wes arrived at his father's farm with news of the bloody battle at Carthage, Jonathan called all his sons together knowing that everyone in the county would soon take sides in the conflict. His family would discover how quickly neighbors could become enemies.

Jonathan Rusk and his wife Nancy moved their young family from Indiana to southwest Missouri in 1838. Like most of their neighbors, they were simple people of the land, innocent in many respects of the powerful drama that nearly a century earlier had been set in motion by a fundamental schism between the promises of the young nation's Constitution and the realities of the life of its people. Thirteen colonial states had defeated the mighty British in the Revolutionary War and a second time in 1812. President Jefferson's Louisiana Purchase vastly expanded the size of the country and paved the way for the birth of a number of new states, but the character of those states had become a matter of heated national debate. Would they join the Union as slave states or free? A deep fault line lay beneath the surface of that westward expansion. The Rusks, the Webbs and their pioneer neighbors were destined to become casualties of a horrific rupture that would split the country in two.

The young nation's Congress had patched together a series of compromises in an attempt to reduce the growing tensions between the North and the South. The South, concerned about political imbalance, had secured a provision in the Constitution that allowed each slave to be counted as three-fifths of a man in the apportionment of its representation. The Fugitive Slave Law of 1793 provided for return to the South of escaped slaves. Both President Jefferson, himself a slave holder, and President John Adams, an opponent of slavery, like many others in the nation, took refuge in the ill-considered expectation that over time slavery would slowly die of its own internal evils. From 1789 forward the Congress provided that free and slave states would be admitted to the Union in pairs, but that balancing arrangement tipped over when Missouri in 1817 demanded that it be admitted as a slave state.

The Compromise Act of 1820, which allowed Missouri to enter the Union as a slave state in conjunction with Maine as a free state, presumed to spread oil on the troubled national waters, but it contained a provision that prohibited slavery from all territory north of the 36/30 parallel with the exception of Missouri. The effect of that provision was to draw an ominous red line separating the North from the South, a line that would turn into a river of blood.

Neither Jonathan nor his Webb neighbors, even if they knew what was happening in Congress, had any sense of the ramifications of such political wrangling about slave and free states. Neither family could have imagined the horrors awaiting them in the years following their arrival in Missouri. Jonathan believed that the corner of the state which touched Kansas, Arkansas and the Indian Territory held great promise for his family. With $100 and a horse he bought his first piece of land soon after they arrived in Jasper County. He quickly threw up a log cabin which his young sons later, their childhood memories overblown, claimed they built with him. Over the next dozen years he kept adding to his acreage. By 1861 he had accumulated over 500 acres and his older sons had settled on sections of it to raise their own families.

Despite the hard life of a pioneer farmer and aspiring cattleman, Jonathan, who was thirty-two when he arrived in Jasper County, now appeared younger than his fifty-five years. He was lean, muscular, over six feet tall and had a dark mustache that curled up slightly at both ends. Of the four sons who were born in Indiana, Reuben, the oldest, was ten when they arrived in Missouri and the youngest, David, was barely a year old.

In the twenty-three years following their arrival the four oldest sons had grown up, married and lived near their father on plots of the Rusk clan's property. All the older sons except David were as tall or taller than their father. Hiram, born in Missouri, was at eighteen nearly as tall as his older brothers, James, the youngest son from his father's first marriage, was a gangly twelve year old. His full name, James K. Polk Rusk, was the result of his being born on January 17, 1849, sixteen days after his father received the deed for a new parcel of land. That document bore the name and seal of the U.S. President, James K. Polk. Jonathan intended his son's name as an honor but for James it was all too often a burden, especially when he got too full of himself and his older brothers called him "Mr. President."

As each of the older brothers arrived that hot muggy July evening to join Wes and their father, they were careful to knock the dirt off their boots before coming inside. Their own mother, Nancy, who had died a few years earlier, was less strict than Julina, their father's second wife. At times they wondered what life had been like for her two previous husbands. The last to appear was David, who never seemed to fit in easily. The shortest of the grown brothers, he was touchy about his height. Unlike one of their rough-spoken neighbors, no one in the family ever referred to David as "the runt of the family," but he was in fact only a tad over five feet and his rounded face further separated him from his brothers who had more angular features.

The greetings that passed around as the brothers all settled in were not as breezy with banter as usual. Each came with his own fears about what might happen to them and their families. Reuben, Wes and John had wives and children and David had just married several weeks earlier.

Julina and Elizabeth Jane, her sixteen year old stepdaughter, whom everyone said looked like her mother Nancy, knew this was "man talk". Together they herded the little ones, Genetti, now six, and her baby brother Walter (already nicknamed "Bud") into the back room. Two baby boys, Thomas and Jonathan Jr., born to Julina between Genetti and Bud, had not survived.

Jonathan tilted his chair back against the stone work next to the hearth as he usually did when the family came together to discuss some serious matter. He tried to convey composure to his sons by slowly, without a word, loading his corn cob pipe with tobacco. He borrowed flame on a straw from the fire, hooked the heels of his tall boots over the front spool of his chair and drew repeatedly on the pipe until smoke began to curl up. It was a small drama that his sons had seen many times before, but none of them, especially the older brothers, took much comfort from it. They were bursting to speak and when their father blew out his first puff, they began talking excitedly over each other. After a few jumbled moments Wes, the second oldest son at twenty eight, broke through the din with his description of the battle he had watched from a safe distance near Carthage that morning. The events of the day had shaken him badly. He feared for his young wife Elizabeth and Mattie, their new born daughter. His voice trembled a bit as he spoke.

"Early this morning I rode over east, Carthage way, to our land near Center Creek to check on a new calf, when I heard thunder and the ground shook. It kept repeating in sudden blasts, not rolling the way thunder does."

Wes tended to be long winded and, although none of his brothers said it, he knew they were all thinking, "Get on with it Wes. We all knew right away it was cannon fire." The booming had shaken the countryside all day, easily penetrating thirty miles or more in every direction from Carthage."

"Well, of course I rode on over that way. The closer I got, the louder the explosions were. I tried to figure out how I could catch sight of the fighting without getting trapped in it."

Jonathan continued puffing out composure as Wes gathered momentum. It was an effort because he had already told much of his tale to the Webb brothers on the way home and several other farmers after that had stopped him to learn what they could. It had been a long frightening day and a lot of time in the saddle. He was almost too tired to talk.

"I found some high ground about nine mile north of Carthage looking off toward Dry Fork, but the smoke from all the musket and cannon fire was so thick across the fields I could hardly make out the fighting. Other farmers who had gathered there before I arrived had bits of information about what had happened. One man said he had heard that Governor Jackson's State Guard had got whupped badly two weeks ago in a skirmish up north at Boonville and had hightailed it south, hoping to get help from regular Confederate troops in Arkansas."

"A second man said he heard that some feren-born Yankee Colonel with a name that sounded like 'seagull' was sent with a company of German troops from St. Louis to cut off Jackson's retreat at Carthage."

David, unable to contain himself, broke in, "Bunch of damned immigrants comin' down here, pointin' their guns at us, tellin' to us how to live our lives."

A quick glance from Jonathan cut him short and Wes continued, "Putting together everything I heard there and on my ride back, it must have been quite a fight. Cannons from both sides blasting back and forth, lines of men with muzzle loaders shooting walls of lead at each other. But I guess Jackson's Missouri men held their ground. How many got killed or wounded I don't know, but some said there were bodies strewn all along the muddy banks of Dry Fork."

Reuben carried the account forward, "Davis, my neighbor to the east, heard that Jackson's men with their hunting rifles and shotguns flanked the Union forces and drove them back into Carthage. It got pretty bad there. The fighting went house to house and the musket and cannon fire damaged a lot of buildings. Word is that the Federals headed off in the direction of Sarcoxie."

Jonathan, who had also heard other accounts and rumors sweeping through the countryside, put his pipe on the table next to him and said, "None of this is much of a surprise, boys. Your mother and I had hardly put up our first log cabin when the fighting back and forth over the Kansas border heated up and I don't need to tell you how it has gotten steadily worse since then. Jawhawkers come across the border to steal Negroes and free them. Missouri men raid Kansas in retaliation with things getting bloodier by the day."

"When crazy old John Brown butchered those people across the border at Potawatomi back in fifty-six and then attacked the arsenal at Harper's Ferry three years later, the die was cast. What happened at Carthage today is just the beginning. Some of our neighbors are already hostile...."

David started to jump in again but Jonathan was not finished and another look in David's direction made that clear. Jonathan picked up his sentence, "They're angry about our support for President Lincoln and us sayin' the South shouldn't be allowed to split the country in two. It's pretty clear we're in the minority and in this county the majority is gonna rule."

"They're not mad at me!" David was almost shouting. The circle of brothers around him kept quiet. His words hung in the air. He started to add more but thought better of it. Jonathan didn't respond.

Wes, a middle brother between Reuben and David was often a peacemaker and felt he understood his temperamental younger brother better than the others. He broke the silence, "I don't know where all this is going, but surely we can keep peace with our neighbors, even those we don't agree with. Take the Webb brothers I spoke with today on the way home. Their family brought their slaves with them when they came up from Tennessee and when Elijah, and his wife died of typhoid a couple of years ago a dozen or more slaves passed to their children. I reckon if you counted up all the slaves in the Webb clan there would be more'n twenty. We don't hold with slavery but I don't think we should be tellin' them or any of our other neighbors how to live their lives."

"Young Willy Webb's slave holdin' kinfolk most likely date way back a couple hundred years, but I'd wager that in his fourteen or fifteen years he's never really thought much about the right or wrong of it."

Reuben, whose comments were usually brief, more like pronouncements than conversation, added, "Like the Good Book says, 'Judge not that ye be not judged.'"

John, the third son, three years younger than Wes and two years older than David, was a bit more given to reflection than his brothers. He said, "Well, there's been a whole lot of judging goin' on and name callin' with it. There ain't many Union folks around these parts what ain't been called "Negra-lovers" or worse. Seems like when trouble starts everybody gets lumped together in some group and callin' people names is the first step down the road to worse things."

"Some people up North and those come out to Kansas who're against slavery and for preservin' the Union lump all us Missourians together and call us 'Pukes.' Couple of weeks ago, a Methodist circuit rider showed me a New York newspaper he brought with him from back east. Article there described what "Puke" means. We're all supposed to be dirt-wallerin' white trash, mostly slavers come up from the south. If anyone caught sight of us they'd see a hairy beast, teeth the color of a walnut, Bowie knife stuck in his belt ready for a fight, bodies a smelly mix of Johnny Cake and badly-smoked bacon, the whole soaked through in whiskey."

Jonathan had heard it all, but for him it was not a time for worryin' about name callin' or for judgments about their neighbors' attitudes. It was a time to make preparation for the dangerous days ahead. He said, "Everyone, includin' each of us, is gonna hafta decide how to deal with the question that might show up at our front door any night–at the end of a barrel."

"I'm not so much worried about people shootin' off their mouths as I am about shootin' lead. I don't know how this country's gonna bridge the gap between the foundin' notion that all men are created equal but some men bein' slaves. What I do know is they're gonna be two sides drawn up now– those who want to save the Union and those who're keen to split off from it. All I can say for now is that we gotta pray to God for peace, but understand that we won't be able to defend ourselves with words alone."

David could no longer be constrained. He jumped to his feet and said, "Well, I sure as hell know what we need to defend ourselves against–the Yankee S.O.B's who attacked Carthage today. They want to shove the Union down our throats and, by Heaven, it won't happen to this Rusk." Before anyone could respond, he was out the front door slamming it behind him.

For what was seconds, but seemed like minutes, no one spoke, then Wes said, "It's just hot-headed Dave. He's all riled up about what's happened today, but he'll cool off." The lack of any response from the others was ominous because they all knew that David had lately been talking a lot with their neighbor, Thomas Livingston, who had brought a troubling reputation with him to the county.

Although the percentage of the population in southwest Missouri that held slaves was much lower than farther north in the counties on both sides of the Missouri River, hostility toward abolitionists was fierce and Lincoln was an object of scorn and hatred. Among the less scurrilous descriptions of him was one printed in the local states rights and secessionist newspaper, C.C. Dawson's "Southwest News." An editorial described him as "six feet four in physical stature and four feet six in mental stature." His northern invaders were promised a welcome "with bloody hands to hospitable graves."

Livingston and his half-brother, William Parkinson, Jr., both slave holders, fit in easily with the majority sentiment in Jasper County. They had come down from Washington County south of St. Louis several years earlier and set up businesses to mine, smelt and transport lead. They also traded goods back and forth between the two counties and on occasion took Indian ponies up to St. Louis.

One of several pieces of land Livingston and Parkinson acquired was just north of Jonathan's main farm. Their five hundred acres was sandwiched east and west between two eighty acre plots of land that Jonathan owned and on its southwest corner touched Wes's land.

The early 1850's were tragic times for Livingston. Two young sons died, a third son was born followed by a daughter, but complications from that birth caused the death of his wife, Nancy, late in the summer of 1853. Livingston left his two surviving children in the care of his widowed mother and travelled back and forth to the newly discovered lead mining area in southwest Missouri. He had been a prosperous landowner in Washington County and with his half-brother saw the prospects for even greater wealth in Jasper County and Newton County. By 1859 their mining operations, both at French Point near Minersville and south a ways in Granby, were going full blast.

One tale that circulated about Livingston had to do with events a few years back at a Presbyterian and Methodist camp meeting ground near Livingston's home up in Washington County. As it filtered down to settlers in the Sherwood area, the story was that Livingston had taken some of his men up to move his belongings south and that, armed and loaded up with whiskey, they descended on the campground causing mayhem at night. They ran wagons and carriages into the river and rode up to where people were eating and let their horses eat off the tables. It was said that Livingston himself went up on the stand and drank whiskey before the religious crowd. Whatever the truth of all that, it was clear around Sherwood and throughout Jasper County that Livingston, not a man to avoid a fight, was a fiery secessionist.

Back at the Webb farm there was much talk about what the next morning would bring. Willy's thoughts had been taking shape and when supper was finished he stood up from the table as tall as he could and said what he felt he had to say. "I'm joinin' up tomorrow!" It wasn't clear to him whether he had said it with enough force to be convincing.

"No you ain't!" James immediately barked back at him. "Over my dead body!"

War talk ended for the night with that declaration, but Willy carried his determination with him to bed. He slept fitfully that night. It was not as though things had been peaceful and sleep always easy before that day. The conflict back and forth over the Missouri-Kansas border had been going on since the family came up from Tennessee and it grew more fierce and bloody with each passing month. The explosions all through that July day were a kind of punctuation to the chaos of several years, ending one sentence and beginning another. What had been bad now threatened to become hellish.

In the dreams that came and went through the night the cannon fire continued and Willy was caught up in the middle of the battle. Cavalrymen raced first one way, then another, through thick clouds of sulfuric smelling gun smoke. Lines of men marched toward each other dropping dead as lead flew back and forth. Suddenly the smoke cleared and he saw Wes Rusk standing over him, pointing a Colt revolver at his head. His panic broke the spell of the dream and he sat straight up in bed, wet with sweat, his heart beating fiercely. He fought falling back into sleep and into the battle. Just as the birds announced that the darkness of morning would soon give way to the rising sun, Willy fell back asleep and was spared any more dreams.

A year after their parents died, James the oldest, who did not already have his own family, was named "Head of Household." He took his responsibility to look after his younger siblings seriously but always with a dash of dry, often sardonic, wit. Annie at 18, a year younger than James, was already a woman. Willy thought fifteen made him a man. Eli, the fragile one, three years younger than Willy, was as attached to Willy as his own shadow. Managing the family farm, even with the help of the thirteen slaves which had passed to James, was a big challenge but he accepted it with sober enthusiasm.

James was never keen on solving problems with guns. He didn't even enjoy hunting and went out after game only when it became necessary. Even if he had felt the need to go to war, he would have never left his brothers and sisters to the care of his older siblings who had children of their own. Willy, by contrast, had nothing to keep him on the farm—not plowing the rocky soil, not pulling up tree stumps, and certainly not mucking out the barn. He remembered the tales of the Mountain Man who had joined the family on their wagon train out of Tennessee and was eager for adventure of his own, even if it involved a bit of danger.

James and Willy fussed back and forth most of the morning of July 6. Finally James stopped arguing. It wasn't that Willy had convinced him. It was not so much that he changed his mind as just stopped objecting. Neither was clear about their roles, but there was a sense that they were both caught up in something bigger than either of them. Willy wasn't quite sure what "fate" meant, but it seemed to have their little family in its grip.

Early that afternoon Willy and James saddled up and headed toward Carthage. James insisted on going along "to check out the damage in town," but also to see what was involved in signing up. As they rode away from the farm, leaving Annie in charge of young Eli, James said, "It may be the name of your horse, Willy, but this ain't gonna be no circus. Some Yankee is gonna fix you in his sights and try to kill yuh. A bullet might come sailin' through the air with your name on it." Willy couldn't think of anything useful to say. He just gave a slight nod of his head which James didn't see.

Carthage, the seat of Jasper County, was a town of about 500 people and most of them seemed to be milling around the square, passing tales back and forth about the drama of the previous day. The Court House, a two story brick building, which in 1854 had replaced an early one room structure, had suffered some serious damage as had the Carthage Academy. Other town buildings had been struck by artillery and musket fire and the strong sulfuric odor of gun powder hung heavily in the air.

As Willy and James rode into the square a number of young women, some just girls, were coming and going from the make-shift hospital set up in the Court House. Two of them passed in front of Circus. As he drew up the younger looking of the two recognized Willy. She called out his name loud enough to embarrass him. "Willy," she said with a touch of gaiety in her voice. It was Myra Maebelle Shirley, daughter of the family who owned the Carthage hotel and saloon. He had met her that spring at a barn dance. Her pretty friend gave Willy a bright smile, but he didn't know who she was.

"You signin' up?" young Miss Shirley said. The gay lilt in her voice suggested that she thought she knew the answer.

"Yep, reckon so," Willy said but his voice sounded neither as manly nor as certain as he intended.

"Did you hear about the Academy bell," Miss Shirley asked, and too eager to wait for his response, she added, "Yesterday a cannon ball rang it when it bounced off the building." Although she and her parents had been hunkered down in their hotel during the fighting, the enthusiasm in her voice and her body language indicated that the dangers and gravity of the day before had not really registered with her. For her it was as though they all had been caught up in an Opera House drama playing the roles assigned to them.

Willy glanced away toward Myra's friend and found she had not taken her eyes off him. Something in her look spoke of composure, self-assurance and maybe more. Did the faintest smile suggest interest in him or was he imagining things? The two passed on by with their baskets of cloth, torn and rolled into strips for bandages. Miss Shirley's friend looked back over her shoulder at him. Willy tipped his hat and watched them as they walked away. When he looked back to James there was the familiar smile on his face that always preceded teasing.

The Confederate regulars in town seemed unconcerned about Union forces returning and on the Court House lawn several tables had been set up as a temporary recruiting station. The men who manned them looked official but hot in their uniforms. Willy and James tied their horses to a hitching post and Willy got in line. James stood out of line but beside him—too big brotherly for Willy's taste.

Willy had been listening to the questions the recruiting officer asked of the three young men in front of him so he was ready when it came his turn. First the basics—his name, where he lived and then the key question, his age. Willy answered that with his best manly voice, "Eighteen Sir."

The recruiter dipped his pen in a silver ink well to the right of his papers, wrote the number slowly then looked up, "Eighteen, you say?"

"Yes Sir, eighteen," firmly answered.

The officer then moved his pen to the "date born" box. His look promised another question, "What day, month and year was that son?"

James leaned into the conversation answering for Willy, "July 2, 1843." He thought to himself, "In for a penny, in for a pound." He too had been listening to the questions asked of the young men ahead of Willy and had made a quick calculation in his head, dropping back three years from 1846. Now was not the time to foul things up for his brother. His express purpose for coming with Willy was to ensure that he signed up for the Regular Confederate forces, not some semi-official guerilla band.

The recruiter had already that day written down several ages that surely were false, but he had his orders from command, "We need soldiers. Sign 'em up!" He smiled at James and looked to Willy for confirmation.

It had taken him a moment to realize what James had done but Willy shifted his weight to the other leg, tried to sound casual and said, "1843, Yes Sir, that was 1843. I was born just four days ago." Then feeling things sliding away from him he corrected, "Well, not born four days ago; it was my birthday just four days ago. Yes Sir, eighteen, born July 2, 1843," eighteen years of age."

The recruiter thought to himself, "And I wasn't born yesterday, either." He stamped several pages, showed Willy where to sign his name, dipped the pen in the silver well again and handed it to James to witness, "Kin, I presume?" Then he signed his own name and rank next to Willy's, slid two pages to his left and handed the third to Willy.

Willy waited a long awkward moment for something else to happen. "What's next, Sir?"

"Next?" The recruiting officer looked up holding back a smile. "Nothing here, son. Take your paper to the table down to the far left and get your assignment."

Willy turned to walk away. James, looking back over his shoulder at the recruiter, skipped a step to get into marching stride with his brother.

"Wait up, son!" came the voice from behind him.

Willy's heart sunk. He turned slowly thinking the jig was up. "The recruiter said, "That your black stallion hitched up over there ?"

"Yes Sir," and with more assurance, "Yes Sir! That's 'Circus.' Raised him from a colt"

"How much you take for him, son?'

This was Willy's first experience with the force of command, something he would encounter constantly for the next four years. He thought for an instant they would confiscate his horse, then gathered himself. "Oh, he's not for sale, Sir. We're a pair. Can't be separated." He waited to be overruled but the recruiter just looked back at his line and called the next recruit forward.

The next step in James' mind was to get Willy and his horse into the Cavalry. Going to war was bad enough, but the thought of Willy trudging along mile after mile with a pack on his back was not something he would accept. At least he thought he could have a say in the matter.

As it turned out the assignment officer had seen Willy and James, both good in the saddle, ride into the Square. He had a keen eye for men and their horses and saw immediately that this lad and his horse would move as one.

Willy handed his paper to the Cavalry officer who flipped over to a new page on his roster, looked up a quick glance at

Willy then back to the roster, scribbled something on Willy's paper and said gruffly without looking up again, "William James Webb, that you?" And before Willy could answer he added, "Command of General Sterling Price. You'll be riding with Captain Jo Shelby and damn lucky to be part of his Brigade!" He handed Willy's paper back. "We're all out of guns for new men. Yuh got one?"

James had always had trouble with authority figures and especially a bore like this military clown. He said, "Be a good idea to have one if you're being sent off to fight, I reckon."

The officer fixed him with a stare which James returned in kind and added only, "Pistol." Willy nodded.

"You know where Cowskin Prairie is?" he asked Willy even more gruffly for James's benefit. Willy wasn't certain, but eager to get past the moment, he nodded, "Yes, Sir."

"Be there in three days, July 9," the officer said and for James' benefit he added, "And bring your pistol."

James had turned to leave but the recruiter held up Willy with one last question. Looking down at Willy's badly worn boots he wearily asked, "Those your best boots, son?"

"No, Sir," Willy answered, paused a second hesitating about what more to say then added crisply in the way he imagined a soldier should respond, "Sir. They're my only boots." The officer shook his head slowly and waived Willy away with a sweep of the back of his hand.

The truth was that the soles were so near to being worn through that James had recently cut some thick leather for insoles and, looking at Willy who had pulled off his dirty socks and was standing barefoot, said, "If the Maker hadn't turned so much of you down for feet, you'd be near seven foot tall." Willy made a sour face and wagged his head slightly from right to left but said nothing. Everyone in the family at one time or another had fun with him about his big feet, narrow with unusually long toes.

On their ride back home Willy had little to say. James broke the quiet, "Havin' second thoughts?"

"No, it's not that," Willy responded. "It just seemed like things should have somehow have been more…more something—more official I guess. Everythin' was so hectic…and casual. Nothing at all classy about it, and it was all over in a few minutes." He thought to himself, "The only thing special was the silver ink well the recruiting officer used. Everything else was rag tag—hot, dirty and disorganized." His voice trailed off, not expecting any response from James and nothing for him to add. They rode on across the prairie a couple of miles before either of them spoke again.

"Pretty girl, huh?" said James.

"Miss Shirley?" Willy responded not wanting to reveal his interest in Myra's friend.

"No, the Vivion girl," James said. "She's the daughter of Julia and John Vivion, lives over Sherwood way. You remember the father. He's the fella was killed in a bad accident. I think it was early in 1856 before we came up from Tennessee. Story has it he was killed hauling timber to build a church over that way. I think it was the Peace Church, the one that lies south off the road past Jonathan Rusk's farm. They say he was driving his twin mules when the king-bolt of the bolster broke, the reach dropped down and he was thrown forward between the mules. They panicked and he was trampled to death. Good, generous, public spirited man they say.

James paused for a reflective moment and added, "Makes one wonder why bad things happen so often to good people, especially when they're doin' God's work? Wife had to raise the children by herself. Girl's name is Eliza, I think. She couldn't have been more than seven or eight when it happened."

Will grunted recognition hoping it was not too evident that, despite the sad family tale, he was pleased to know her name. "Eliza," he repeated in his mind and the name melded with an image of her warm but constrained smile. He would pick James' brains later to learn more about her and her family, but for the moment the name was enough to savor.

Willy changed the subject. "About the gun, James. I wasn't sure what gun you meant when the Cavalry officer asked. I can't take anything you'll need at the farm." Both of them knew he was not referring to squirrel hunting or killing coyotes, but rather the danger from Jayhawkers that made everyone fearful, especially at the sound of horsemen in the night. More than one neighbor's slaves had been stolen and taken across the border to be freed in Kansas and some of the slave owners had been killed in cold blood.

"It's father's Colt revolver I had in mind," said James. "The one he bought at the general store when we stopped in Springfield on our way up to Jasper County. I hid it away after he died. J.C. asked about it several times but I played dumb, said I had no idea what happened to it. I knew if he laid hands on it neither of us would see it again." He added, "Looks to me like if they want yuh to fight they'd supply the guns. What more they expect yuh to bring I'm not sure, but maybe we can scare up some sort of rifle in the family".

Willy's mind had stopped at his father's Colt. The thought of taking it off to war troubled him and put him in mind of what his father had taught him about guns back in 1858. One of their neighbors to the east had been killed by night riders who dragged him out in the night and shot him for no reason. Elijah had called his sons together the next day to talk once again to them about the mounting dangers and the urgency of being ready to defend themselves and their families. As a family having more slaves than many of their southern neighbors in the area, they knew they were targets for the Jayhawkers. The older boys had their own guns and knew how to use them. Willy had only done some squirrel hunting.

Early the same evening after the chores were done, Elijah had taken a box from under his bed and unwrapped the cloth protecting a handsome leather holster. He called Willy to join him. They sat on a low stone wall in front of the cabin. Willy remembered that back in Springfield on the last leg of their long on trip up from Overton County when his father came come out of the trading post he hid something in his pocket. He hadn't heard his father tell James how much it cost, an extravagant fourteen dollars, and explain that they wouldn't be telling his mother about it.

With what to Willy seemed almost like reverence his father unsnapped the flap of the leather holster and slowly slid the pistol out. It was his most prized possession, a Colt Model 1851 Navy Revolver. He showed Willy the engraved cylinder on which there was a miniature scene depicting a battle between the Texas and Mexican navies. Around the front edge of the cylinder in letters almost too small to read it said "ENGAGED 16 MAY 1843". No one but Elijah had ever fired it, but now Willy was being taught how to care for it–how to load, shoot, and keep it clean. Willy was not sure he would remember later the steps for loading–combustible cartridges into the cylinders, leave one cylinder empty for safety, the hammer on rest, caps in last.

In the woods a couple hundred yards from the cabin Elijah set up a bottle on a stump and handed the pistol to Willy, "Let's see what you can do, son," When Willy aimed and squeezed the trigger he was surprised by the kick back. The first shot hit a tree next to the bottle. Shattered glass finally marked the fourth shot. Confident now and feeling playful Willy mindlessly pointed the pistol at their hound dog.

Now, nearly three years later, his father's quick and sharp admonishment rang in his ears, "You'll only hear this from me once, Willy. Never point a gun at anythin' or anyone unless you're prepared to shoot!"

Willy tried unsuccessfully to imagine pointing a gun at one of his friends or neighbors. Some of them would most likely be as willing to fight for the Union cause as he was to defend his family's property and way of life. But now he was a fighter. Fighters shoot people and get shot at, no escaping that. He had joined the Confederate Cavalry–he and Circus. The import of that had been slowly building in his mind and now, up in his loft bed with the house quiet, it took full shape. He felt quite different but it wasn't something he could have explained easily to anyone. Yesterday he was a boy. Now he was a man and the transformation had taken place in just a few hours. He was leaving the farm, going off to he knew not where, to do he knew not what, but he was a man in the going.

Intertwined with those thoughts and images was a second swirl of images–images of a girl, Eliza, and they were different from any other thoughts he had ever had about a girl. He guessed that she might be fourteen, maybe even just thirteen, but the sense of her age was as different to him as his sense now of himself. The drama of the last two days left no one his age the luxury of remaining a child. His recollection of Eliza's smile, how she fixed her gaze on him and the grace of her movement as she walked away with her friend, Myra, slid with his consciousness into lovely dreams, dreams also different from a boy's dreams. The next morning those powerful images and feelings lingered in his mind and body as he woke, and the lingering kept him from going quickly down to breakfast when Annie called up to him. There was embarrassment to avoid with Annie and even more with James, who was always prone to see the humor in things. Young Eli would probably not have noticed.

The day would be full of things to do before heading off the following morning for Cowskin Prairie, but even more important than gathering stuff up for his kit, Willy was determined to leave time that afternoon for a ride over to where Eliza lived near Sherwood. His plan was to be casual, pretend he was "just in the area" and see her before he left for training. It was the plan of a boy who had not yet escaped the shyness of an adolescent and not yet arrived at the certain desires of manhood. He had thought about a letter, but decided that would be too direct and feared that she might not even remember who he was. He hoped Eliza would think he was gallant and would promise to write to him.

Willy had put together some essentials for his kit and was trying to figure out how to pack his violin when he heard

James shout, "Willy, grab those 'cow belly things' from the barn and come quick out to the south field. Cows have gotten into the alfalfa."

"Cow belly things?" Willy shouted back.

"Yeh, looks like a giant nail hollowed out. Has a sharp tip. And bring our wooden mallet."

Willy knew what James was describing, but had never known what it was called or what it was for. In the field he found James with three of their best milk cows. They were lying on their sides in the alfalfa field with huge, swollen bellies.

James, who was usually calm and collected, was in a panic. He kneeled down at the cow's head and said, "I'll hold her down. You take that thing, put it about half way down on her belly between two ribs and drive it in hard." Willy feared he would kill her, but James' directions were urgent.

James cautioned, "Lean to one side when you drive it in." Willy placed the sharp point between two ribs and swung the mallet hard. He regretted not leaning further away when, with a whoosh, the belly gas blew out a stream of green slime. The procedure had the same effect with the two other cows. Their breathing slowly began to ease. Willy and James stayed with them through the afternoon until the drains stopped running and all three cows were able to stand.

It was only as they led the cows back to the barn that Willy realized the afternoon was gone and with it any hope of seeing Eliza before he left the next morning for Cowskin Prairie. It was easily an eight to ten mile ride round trip over to her family's place, the sun was already setting, and he still had most of his packing to do. There would surely be letters from his family but not the sort he had imagined from Eliza.

Back in the house after an early dinner, Willy climbed back up to the loft to finish putting his kit together. James climbed up after him to check out the effort, found Willy wrapping his bedroll around his violin case and asked, "You're gonna lug around your fiddle?"

Willy grunted, "Yup," but added nothing more in the pause that followed.

"Not a bad idea," James said, totally deadpan, "If you can't kill the Yankees with your gun, you can slay them with your fiddlin'!" James was not musical but had a way with words and had deliberately picked the word "slay." He was, however, not surprised that Willy saw the fiddle as an essential part of his limited gear. It was the rare day when he didn't play it. James had seen how making music had helped Willy get through the sudden loss of both of their parents. Maybe it would also help him get through the war. He clearly had inherited their father's musical talent and in the past year had been much sought after to play at barn dances.

Willy got the joke, which for a moment cut through the apprehension that was filling the cabin that evening, but there would be no gay tunes that night. No one else in their little family knew that part of the gloom was Willy's disappointment that he hadn't had a chance to call on Eliza.

CHAPTER FIVE

Willy's siblings gathered round him as he finished securing his kit behind Circus' saddle. Several of their slaves had come to say goodbye but were hanging back. Willy walked over to them and shook hands with Old Peter and Jack, taking each man's hand in both his hands. Old Peter thought to himself, "Shame this young'un's signin' up with the wrong side. Ain't even got a clear notion in his head what he's gonna fight for." Next to him were Julia and her two children, Harriet and Granville. They were the slaves Willy's father most favored. Harriet stood half behind her mother and giggled quietly. Granville, now seven and tall for his age, was the first to speak. With a big smile he said, "Bye, Massuh Willy." Julia, now thirty-five, was in the prime of her womanhood. He had never done it before but, to her surprise, Willy kissed her cheek. It was wet with tears.

Hugs and kisses from his sisters, a firm handshake from James and the same from Eli, imitating James rather than his sisters, sent Willy on his way. Without realizing it they had made an unspoken agreement with each other. Together they formed a choir of constraint, not wanting their emotions to distress him.

Willy's destination to the south was Cowskin Prairie, which lay in the extreme southwest corner of Missouri, a scant few miles from Arkansas on the south and Indian Territory on the west.. He felt both the adventurer's excitement and apprehension at what he was getting himself into. James' warning that men would "fix him in their sights and try to kill him" kept echoing in his mind. At moments he felt like a boy caught up in a silly prank, but at other moments he was a man going off to fight for the Confederacy and all that was precious to Southerners. "Fight" for him then was still a pristine concept, not stained by anyone's blood, especially not his own.

The first day's ride went well and the next morning, after a breakfast of the biscuits and hardtack his sisters had packed for him, he heard the sound of horses coming his way down the trail. He pulled Circus in with him behind some trees fearing it was a Yankee patrol, but as the riders came in sight he recognized them. They were two of his cousins, Benjamin Franklin Hatcher who liked to be called "Benjie," and Thacker Vivion Webb.

"Mornin' Thack, hey Benjie," Willy said stepping out into the open. "Reckon you're goin' off down to Cowskin Prairie like me and Circus." Benjie was tall like his father, Jabez Tall Hatcher, the husband of Willy's sister Paulina, the oldest of his siblings. He had a shotgun on his back, held there by a leather strap that ran across his bony chest. He was wearing a ridiculous slouch hat that looked like a horse had sat on it. Thack had a way of looking like his clothes were always newly store-bought. Willy found him the odd one out among his cousins. He was always talkin' about family that lived way back in the early times in Virginia. Willy's mother had explained that Thack's father and grandfather had the same preoccupation, so it was something young Thack couldn't have easily avoided.

Two and a half hard day's ride brought the three boys into the training camp at Cowskin Prairie. A motley group of men, all ages and states of dress, milled around among the tents and campfires. Groups here and there were playing cards. Others were riding their horses around on the fringe of the tent area, where many wagons were located. One clownish man was riding a large black mule. The thought "circus" came to Willy's mind but he dutifully suppressed it, after all he was now a shur'nuff Confederate soldier.

A young man wearing a uniform, unlike many others, spoke to the Webb boys. "Howdy. You men just git in?" "Men" had a nice ring to it, trying as hard as they were to be grown up.

Willy spoke for them, "Come down from north of here, Jasper County." The man who had bestowed manhood on them so effortlessly had a drawl that to Willy suggested more west than south. He said his name was Curtis Jackson.

"Everyone calls me 'C.J.' Been away at school back East. Jest come back for the summer to my folk's place west of Waco, Texas, when this ruckus between the north and south broke loose. I'm signed up with Brigadier General Ben McCullough. We're made up of men from Texas and

Louisiana. Linkin' up here with the militia of your Missouri Governor Jackson and Major General Price—that's Sterling Price, who back some years was also your Governor." Seeing the newcomers were overwhelmed by all the command stuff and names, C.J. added, "Not to worry, you'll figure out who all the top men are right soon."

Although it seemed to Willy that C.J. was enthusiastic about soldierin', it was a decision that he had deliberated about for days. He told Willy that he had been back East for two years studying history and philosophy at a school called Harvard. He found Boston, and Cambridge, the town across the Charles River where Harvard was, to be lively, stimulating places. He quickly felt at home there. The tipping point about the war for C.J. was a sense of duty to his home state, not unlike that for General Robert E. Lee who, rumor had it, passed up the job as head of the whole northern army to fight instead for the South and his home state Virginia.

Training at Cowskin prairie was a whirl of largely disorganized activity. Willy had signed up for the cavalry, so the marching drill seemed pointless to him. What stood out from the other training activity was what he learned about how to use a gun. C.J. told Willy to turn his pistol holster around so that the butt of the handle faced forward. C.J. demonstrated how to hold the horse's reins in the left hand, reach over them with his right hand and in one sweep draw the pistol and point it forward.

"That won't do for me," Willy said.

"What's that again?" C.J. asked.

"I'm left handed," replied Willy.

C.J. laughed, "Just switch it opposite mine."

Through most of the rest of the afternoon, riding Circus out beyond the tent area, he practiced the action. Reins in right hand. Draw pistol with left hand over the reins. Fire. The last bit was pretend but Willy had a growing sense that would not be for long.

A second gun lesson came that night after supper as C.J., a couple of his Texan friends, and the three Missouri boys sat together. To Willy it sounded more like a history lesson than army stuff. C.J. told them how important it was for cavalrymen to learn what he called the "partin" shot. Riding away fast from a battlefield, you loop the reins around the saddle horn and twist your body around facing backward to look and fire your rifle back at the enemy. "That way," C.J. explained, "you can fight as hard retreatin' as you can chargin.'" He added, "It's actually called the 'Parthian' shot after some ancient warriors in Asia who developed it as a bow and arrow horseback shot hundreds of years ago." Sounded sensible to Willy, but he didn't own a rifle. Many of the men in camp had shotguns and squirrel rifles, but others had no weapons at all. It was that night that some of the other men listening in from nearby gave C.J. the nickname, "Professor."

A less book-learned teacher was Thack, whose tales were told mostly to his Webb cousins, with C.J. sometimes listening in. His favorite story was how their Webb ancestors intermarried with some famous Virginia people a couple of hundred years earlier. Long before the Revolution, when Virginia belonged to the British, according to his account, there was a Captain Giles Webb, their ancestor many generations back. He married a rich widow named Randolph and his land together with hers made up over seven thousand acres. Willy and Benjie found that hard to believe. The Randolphs, Thack explained, along with the Jefferson's had been famous Virginians from the late 1600's until now.

"You mean Jefferson, like President Thomas Jefferson?" Benjie said incredulously.

"Yup, as God is my witness," replied Thack. "They been marryin' back and forth ever since."

"So you're sayin' we're kin to Thomas Jefferson," puzzled Willy.

"You betcha," answered Thack. "Ain't it a kick?"

On July 25 the camp was a whirl of excitement. General Price had made his first big decision, to march up into Missouri and take the state from the Federals. General McCullough, who had a separate command, coordinated his strategy with Price. Their objective was Springfield, where a combination of southern forces would meet up for a big attack. Different routes up were taken. The command under which Willy and his cousins rode took the more western route, which by the second day placed them near a village called Medoc, not far from the Webb land, two days ride east and a bit south of Springfield. Their bivouac had been set up for an hour when, just after sundown, a lone rider came into camp, cleared by their pickets. It was frail skinny looking youth, most likely a local courier bringing information about the location of Federal troops. Swinging down to the ground, the rider took off his broad brimmed hat, and shook out a long brown head of hair. To everyone's astonishment the him was a her. "That's her," someone said, "That's Eliza." Another said her last name sounded like "whizzin'." Over the laughing another voice said with authority, "It's "Vivion." The sound of her name could not have had more force for Willy if it had been the clang of a big bell right next to his ear. "Eliza!"

As bits and pieces of information were shared around the picture sharpened. Her older brother, Newton, rode with Tom Livingston's band. She was the granddaughter of Thacker Vivion, the first white man into that part of Missouri. She was only thirteen and it was said she could sit a horse as well as any man and took fences fearlessly, often riding on dark moonless nights, forging swollen streams to follow the shortest route out and back home.

Eliza had huddled with the officers for no more than a quarter hour when the group broke up and one of the officers said, "Who here knows this countryside well enough to escort this young woman home?" Several hands went up. Willy was the nearest to the officer. He jumped to his feet, waving his hand in the air. "You, young fella," the officer pointed to Willy, "and don't meander on the way back. There's Federals out there." A moan went up from the others, several of whom were still waving their hands in the air.

Sometimes the dice roll in your favor, sometimes you draw the card you need. This was one of those moments when fortune steps in and spins one's life around. Eliza was up on her horse and off before Willy could focus. It was fifty yards before he and Circus caught up with her. She rode fast with great confidence, taking the occasional split rail fence on some farmer's land without breaking stride. Willy was glad there was a full moon that night. It not only lit their path, but created just the right ambience.

After half an hour they stopped at a stream to water their horses. Willy spoke first. "Ain't your folks worried when you're out like this."

"Well, my Pappy's been dead several years. It started out simple, me takin' a message and letters now and then to my brother, Newton. Somehow it jest grew from there. Mother was dead set against it at first, but one thing led to another and before long I was watchin' how the Federals moved around the county and reportin' that to any Confederates in the area. Sometimes I'd carry officer's messages to each other, and sometimes family letters to the men. Guess I'd have to say I like excitin' things."

Eliza had seemed more than a girl when he first saw her on the day he signed up, and now he was talking to a woman. It was a short ride on to the Vivion farm, which lay just north of a bend in Center Creek a bit west of Sherwood, one of the larger villages in the county. Fate had not allowed that ride weeks earlier the night before he left for Cowskin Prairie, but was blessing Willy now.

A lamp shone in the front of the Vivion cabin as Willy and Eliza rode up. She dropped down from her horse. Willy followed and took off his hat. Wrapping her horse's reins around a fence rail, Eliza stepped up close in front of him. She said, "Willy Webb, Willy Webb," as if there was a problem to be solved. "Willy's a boy's name," she declared as she reached up, took his face in her hands and kissed him full on the lips, holding it longer than was her first impulse. "Now you're 'Will.'" Her declaration had the ring of finality. "Yes, I like that, 'Will.'" And with that she turned and started toward the barn, leading her horse. Will, frozen in place for a moment, gathered himself and said, "Will I see you again?" Opening the door to the barn, she answered without looking back, "I'll make sure of it."

There was nothing then for Will, the new person, to do but mount up and ride off. His first thought was, "If this is the alternative to war, why am I heading back to camp?" The ride was long enough for Will to let his excitement subside. He knew he would be ragged badly enough when he got back, without that embarrassment. And true to expectation there were hoots and jeers and assorted crude comments when he rode in. As a diversion, he sought out Thack to ask him a question that had been on his mind since the day he met Eliza and now had a special relevance. "Your name is the same as Eliza's grandfather, Thack," he observed. "You and Eliza related?"

"From way back," Thack answered, "and so are you."

"Me, what?"

"Related. Yup. The Thackers, Vivions and Webbs," he explained, have been marrying each other, mixing and matching names for a couple hundred years."

Leaving that news to ponder later, Willy said, "Speakin' of names, I wish you'd all call me 'Will.' Little boys are called 'Willy.'"

Sensing that this meant something more to Willy than appeared on the surface, C.J. quickly spoke up before the request was batted around. He said with authority, "'Will,' that's exactly what it should be—great name for a warrior, rhymes with 'kill.'" C.J.'s intent was light hearted, but the word "kill" hung in the air. It was an augury of something that everyone knew was waiting for them at Springfield, now only about two days ride away.

The Confederate forces now under the single command of General McCullough, included, along with the local Mis-

souri State Guardsmen, men from Texas, Louisiana, and
Arkansas, some full-blooded Indians from Indian Territory
and some with mixed blood. As they moved along Telegraph
Road, closing on their destination, Will sensed a growing confidence among the men as their numbers swelled. There were
different counts of the total, but the best reckoning he had
heard was upwards of six thousand cavalry, over five thousand infantry and a dozen or more pieces of artillery. Added
to that were some two thousand Missouri State Guardsmen,
unarmed, but ready to fight somehow.

Travel through their last day had an eerie feeling. As they
moved over a long series of rolling hills, a heavy fog settled in
making it hard to see even twenty yards ahead down the trail.
It was the sixth of August, a month and four days after Will's
fifteenth birthday. He had been in the cavalry for thirty-two
days. Encampment was made for the night along Wilson's
Creek, ten miles southwest of Springfield. By sundown the
fog that had shrouded the afternoon's march had turned to
drizzle. The Confederate attack on the town was planned for
the night of August 9, but had to be postponed because the
gunpowder that men carried in untreated canvas bags, or just
in their trouser pockets, was too damp to fire.

As night fell the Webb men, C.J., and two of his fellow
Texans were coaxing their fire. Its damp kindling was sending
up more smoke than flame. Two men joined them. "Evenin,"
said one. "Name's Frank." The other said, "I'm Edwards."
The conversation that unfolded back and forth reflected the
variety of attitudes among the men who had come to fight.

Frank, the younger of the two newcomers, spoke with
great animosity about the Federals. "My little brother who's
fourteen, four years younger than me, was set upon by some

Union sympathizers. They thought he knew where Quantrill was and when he had nothin' to tell them they whupped him and left him bleedin' out in our field. When he dragged himself to the house, he found the men had strung up our stepfather while Mother watched, horrified. Jesse was able to cut him down and he lived but his breathin' had stopped for too long. His mind had turned to mush. Our mother and sister were arrested and put in prison at St. Joe. Sis caught malaria there. The boy's seethin' with anger, wants to join up right away with Quantrill. I'm tellin' him he's too young."

Will had heard of the guerilla Quantrill and his fierce reputation. He asked Frank, "What did you say your kid brother's name was?"

"Jesse," Frank answered, "Jesse James."

C.J. who was sitting directly across the fire from Frank said, "Friend, you're sweatin' and flushed in the face. You comin' down with somethin'?"

"Yeh, reckon so," Frank answered, it's been creepin' up on me all day."

At the mention of Quantrill the guerilla leader, Edwards, who had been jotting notes in what looked like a diary, launched into an enthusiastic and long-winded paean of the rebel's adventures.

When the group broke up, C.J. confided to Will, "I get troubled when I hear brutal men like Quantrill glorified and all the talk in general about the glory of war. Even when more thoughtful men speak of the evils of war, I'm reminded of what one of my professors up at Harvard liked to say—that we tell our children about the horrors of war, but they see the gleam in our eye."

In Springfield the Connecticut Yankee General, Nathaniel Lyon, had assembled a force of over sixty-four hundred men. It was made up of U.S. Army Regulars, Missouri Union men, many of whom were recent immigrants from Germany, and volunteers from Kansas and Iowa. Lyon's scouts had brought back reports of the large Confederate force assembling to their south. He decided on a surprise attack. Leaving behind a thousand men to hold the town and guard their supplies, Lyon mounted his assault before sunrise on the 10th.

Will and his Webb cousins were huddled together sheltering from the rain, when at 5:00 A.M. the war came crashing down upon them. Exploding artillery shells sent men, tents and equipment flying in every direction. Supply wagons, with their mules still hitched to them, were incinerated by fireballs. Will ran for Circus and saw C.J. leap on his horse ahead of him. Out there were the Federals, the men who would fix him in their sights.

Will heard the thundering fusillades from his side as they began to answer the North. Orders rang out from Southern officers bringing order out of chaos. Through the morning hours of close combat, repeated Confederate charges slowed the Federal advance and then began to drive them back. A little over six hours after the first shots were fired by the North, overwhelmed by the tenacity of the South and their superior numbers, they retreated to Springfield.

By noon the sun had burned off the fog and the drizzle had stopped. Will found himself in the midst of a battlefield still shrouded in smoke from cannon and small arms fire. Men from both sides were scattered around him where they had fallen. Most lay still, but cries for help came from a few survivors. It was midday, but it seemed to Will like he had just awakened from a nightmare of sights and sounds. He knew he had been shot at and that he had fired his pistol several times, and it was more like a drama he had witnessed than one in which he was a player. The battle had both gone on forever and at the same time passed in a flash.

The sound of C.J.'s voice helped him focus. "Bless God, you made it, Will," he said. Will couldn't think of what to say. Together they started back in the direction of their camp. C.J. was riding slightly ahead when he realized that Will was not with him. Looking back, he saw that Will had dismounted and was looking down behind a large boulder. As C.J. rode up beside Will he could see what caught his attention. Behind the boulder was a Federal soldier, a Negro, lying where he had been hit. He wore a new pair of boots and beside him, with his hand still gripping it, was a shiny new rifle. C.J. freed the rifle from its owner's fingers and handed it to Will. "You saw it first." he said. But Will was still looking down.

"Right." C.J. added. "It's the boots. Good'n long, like your feet." From the day they first met in Prairie Grove C.J. had been wondering how long Will's shabby boots would last. "Pull 'em off and let's git out of here" he urged Will. "Can't be sure the Federals won't attack again."

It helped for Will to be given orders. Otherwise, he might not have mustered the will to do what other Southern men were doing around the battlefield. He shoved the rifle into the roll behind Circus' saddle and bent down to the fallen soldier. Getting the boots off was not easy and at one point, pulling hard, he imagined the Union man was still alive. Up on Circus, with the boots shoved between him and the saddle horn, he and C.J. made their way back to their company.

Will fended off a number of handsome bids for the rifle. When word got around about who the former owner of the boots was, they drew only a few offers. After some beans, hard tack and black coffee, Will sat by the campfire, boots off, feet toward the fire, socks now dry. The new boots stood together at attention behind him.

Although none of the others who had gathered around the fire had taken any notice, C.J. discerned what was going on in Will's mind. He nudged Will over, sat in beside him and said, "I was rememberin' what Thack said about you Webbs bein' related to the Jeffersons eons ago." When Will looked over at him C.J. paused for effect, then added, "Brought to mind what old Thomas Jefferson said in the Declaration of Independence about feet." That drew the attention of everyone in the group.

"Feet?" Will puzzled. "Feet in the Declaration of Independence?"

"Sure." C. J. said with authority. "We hold these truths to be self-evident that all feet are created equal."

Some chuckled, others hee-hawed. Not everyone got the point. To Will there was a gentle rebuke in his friend's humor and the hint of a larger truth that he only partly grasped, a truth that hovered above the war. The next morning Will pulled on the boots. They fit.

Spirits were high among the Confederates about their first major victory in Missouri. Rumors had it that the Union General, Lyon, was killed shortly before the Federals retreated. There were estimates that as many as twelve to thirteen hundred Union men were killed, wounded or missing. It, however, had also been a costly battle for the Confederates, for whom the grizzly casualty count was nearly as bad–more than twelve hundred and it all had taken place in less than six hours. It was hard for Will to get his mind around the extent of death and gruesome injuries. More than once he suppressed vomit at the sight of a comrade's wounds. He kept his distance from the bloody sights and painful cries of the hospital tent, where arms and legs had to be amputated. Will knew he had fired and reloaded his pistol many times, but wasn't sure whether he had killed anyone or not. How he made it through himself seemed a miracle. It was all he could do at times to control Circus with shells exploding on all sides.

A Lieutenant named Blackwell moved among the men that morning to praise their toughness and cheer them on. He said to Will, "Suspect you saw the elephant out there yesterday mornin'."

"Elephant, Sir?" Will puzzled.

The officer explained with a smile,"You mean you didn't see ole General Hannibal's brigade and his elephants out there yesterday? Can't figure how a man could miss that." Over his shoulder as he walked away he added, "Handsome rifle you picked up, son." Will watched as the Lieutenant moved on down the line speaking to his men. The only Hannibal he knew of was a town way up the Mississippi from St. Louis. He couldn't imagine that they raised elephants there; maybe mules. C.J., taking pity, leaned toward Will and said in a low voice, "You got shot at yesterday for the first time, didn't you Will? Well, that's what 'seein' the elephant' means."

The rifle was admired by everyone who saw it. Will daily turned down offers as high as fifty dollars for it but, in bits and pieces, he learned why it was so highly prized. It was an 1860 model Henry repeating rifle, brass

frame and twenty-four inch blued octagonal barrel. It used
.45 caliber self-contained brass cartridges and its lever
action allowed for sixty shots a minute. One man, who
seemed to be an expert on guns, said it was developed from
the design of a man by the name of Henry Tyler at one of
those big gun companies up in the northeast. He was surprised to see one in use already. Word had it that it wasn't
going to be on the market for another year or more. As luck
would have it, cartridges for it were found in one of the
Union supply wagons they had just captured. Another
would-be buyer explained its powerful appeal, "With it, one
man's as good as fourteen men with single shot rifles. You
load it on Sunday," he exclaimed, "and shoot all week!"

The Confederate victory at Wilson's Creek, a month
after its earlier victory at Carthage, was followed by a dramatic victory at Lexington, one-hundred miles north on the
Missouri River. Success had swollen the force with new
recruits. Will was caught up in the exuberance of the more
than ten thousand men who marched on the river town.
They overwhelmed Lexington's three thousand Union
defenders, who surrendered on September 20 after a dramatic siege. Control of the whole state seemed only a few
battles away, but winter was coming on and the tide was
about to turn.

The men under Price's command had marched back to
Springfield to winter and recoup there. Willy pitied the
infantrymen who had, on the drive to Lexington and back,
slogged along for nearly three-hundred miles. Even on horseback it was a grueling march. And arriving in Springfield,
the Confederate men learned there were miles yet to go.

Yankee forces were threatening, and General Price decided to move his forces back into Arkansas for safety. Some of the Texans tried to convince Will that it would be warmer there, but he saw little difference.

The color of the Arkansas autumn gave way to the grim cold of winter. At the end of February news spread through the camp that Union forces were advancing toward them and that a new Confederate commander, General Earl Van Dorn, had arrived. Thack, who had passed that news to Willy added, "And have yuh heard? We got a new name. Now we're called 'The Army of the West.'" It sounded grand to Willy, but the bitter cold put frost on its shine.

Van Dorn was not a man to sit and wait for the fight to come to him. On the day after his arrival he assembled his troops and marched north out of the Boston Mountains to surprise the Union forces under the command of General Samuel Curtis. Two days march brought the Confederates to Bentonville and the valley of Little Sugar Creek.

In camp that night, the sixth of March, word passed around that they would be moving out early the next morning heading further north. C.J. said to Will, "I think I see what our new General's plan is. He's gonna try to get us up around north of the Yanks, attack them from behind and take control of Telegraph Road, their supply line from the north." Will had already guessed the same. He was getting the hang of battle plans. Circus was also more seasoned–the horrendous sounds of battle spooked him less.

Van Dorn was not able to attack at sunrise. Neither Price nor McCullough's large supporting contingents had arrived. Having lost the element of surprise, Van Dorn divided his forces and drove south, coming in on the Yankees from both the right and left. The Army of the West collided with the Union forces just before 10:00 AM at one location near an inn called Elkhorn Tavern and at a second near a village called Leetown, the other side of Round Top Mountain. Will, his Webb cousins and C.J. fought with the troops at Round Top Mountain. With them was General Pike's fierce brigade of Indians from Indian Territory, west of the Arkansas border. Will had seen a lot of bloody fighting at Wilson's Creek, but when he saw the Indians taking Yankee scalps it turned his stomach.

The battle raged back and forth, each side at times advancing or retreating. Will, for the first time used the "Parthian shot" C.J. had taught him, turning to fire when in retreat, the lever action of his Henry sending back a stream of lead. Several Confederate officers were killed before the first day's fighting ended. Among them was General McCullough himself, downed by a Yankee sharpshooter. Returning to camp at dusk, Will remembered how his father, on the day he taught him how to fire the Colt, said he had never shot at a man. Will could no longer say the same, and he hadn't missed.

The second day's battle focused on Elkhorn Tavern. The artillery of Brigadier General Franz Siegel, the Union General second-in-command to Curtis, pounded the Confederates assembled at the base of a large rise in the land called Pea Ridge. Will, who carried a bandolier of Henry cartridges around his chest, heard repeated cries for more ammunition from men around him and his side's artillery fire slowed in its pace. The Confederate supply wagons had to come around a long haul of rough roads and had taken a wrong turn at one point. They never reached Price or Van

Dorn, who now knew he had to retreat. Using a deceptive move, he pulled the main body of his forces off the battlefield and escaped to the south. By the end of the day Will, riding among ranks of exhausted and wounded men, arrived safe in Van Buren, Arkansas. The Confederates knew that in their defeat they had taken a heavy toll on the Yanks, but their losses were even greater. Only after a few days was the extent of their defeat known—over a thousand men killed and wounded with three hundred or more captured.

It was only as the months of 1862 passed that Will came to understand that the battle at Pea Ridge was a major turning point in the war, a monumental defeat for the Confederates west of the Mississippi. From that point on well into 1863 the main action was harassing Union forces back up in Missouri, attacking supply trains, and from time to time, a pitched battle. Will was now a hardened veteran, but his conviction that anything very useful was being done by such sporadic fighting was waning. C.J.'s occasional comments reflected even more serious doubts.

In early January, 1863, Springfield, the major supply base of the Union in southwest Missouri, was targeted a second time for a Confederate raid. It was a bold move intended to turn the tide of the war back in the South's favor. Three Confederate columns made their way north out of Arkansas, following separate routes. Will was pleased to learn his contingent would pass through the southwest corner of Jasper County. It was near his home, but even more promising, it was the area where Eliza had pursued her courier activities.

Had he stacked the cards for that night's events himself, it could not have turned out better for Will. No sooner had their bivouac been set up for the night near Carthage, when he heard the sound of their sentry bringing a rider with him into camp. Ten of Spades. It was a frail looking youth. Jack of Spades. Long brown hair flowing down when the slouch hat came off. Queen, same suite. A glance in his direction as he moved nearer the officers and Eliza huddled with them. King of Spades. Eliza standing beside the senior officer pointed to Will. Ace, black–again the right suit!

The ride that night toward Sherwood and the Vivion farm followed a different route than the first time. Will and Eliza rode at a casual pace, each telling the other what had happened in the intervening months. The last words he had heard from Eliza the night of their first meeting, in response to his hope to see her again, had repeated in his mind dozens of times, "I'll make sure of it." She had now made it happen and without anything specific said to support his hope, he knew they were equally drawn to each other, and it was not the attraction of teenagers. They both had been driven into adulthood by the war and as young people in wartime often do, they sought to fulfill their desires lest there be no opportunity later. Inside the Vivion barn, Eliza, whose young life had already seen great tragedy, told Will that her brother, Newton, riding with Livingston, had been killed two weeks earlier. She sobbed as she shared her fears of what would befall her family next and moved forward a short step into Will's arms. That embrace opened the door to the need for love that both of them felt and set loose the passion that surged beneath it. Both of them were inexperienced in the ways of love making. Each movement seemed easy and natural, but it all passed more quickly than either of them wished as their bodies shuddered together in a moment more delicious than either of them could have anticipated.

They lay in each other's arms on a blanket padded beneath by a soft pallet of straw, dreading their parting, but knowing that Will was already overdue back at his camp. Both were quiet and subdued in their parting kiss. Goodbyes put into words too often were prophecies of bad things to come so they conspired to end the night with silent waves to each other as Will rode off toward his camp. It was late enough when he arrived that almost everyone in the camp was asleep, so he escaped the rude comments and was able to fall asleep himself, swimming in the memories of moments too precious for words to capture.

The next morning, January 8, arrived with the harshness of battlefield expectations and the chill of a cold wind. It was a short ride to Springfield. As the Confederate columns merged, they knew the Yankee scouts would have carried word of their approach and good estimates of their two thousand man force. The Union General, Egbert Brown, had been tempted to destroy all his supplies and mount a full retreat, but took courage and prepared aggressively for the onslaught. Enrolled Missouri Militia were summoned from the surrounding area and civilians were armed. Brown even burned some homes to clear a line of fire south from Fort Four, one of four earthen forts, each commanding high ground.

The three men of the Webb clan, C.J., and his Texan comrades were all now battle hardened members of what had come to be called "The Iron Brigade," led by Colonel Jo Shelby. For their first assault, they were ordered to dismount and move across the open fields, using rock piles, tree trunks and what was left of burned homes for cover. The assault on Fort Four failed and another Confederate attack followed. Pushing the Federals back to College street, the combat was fierce, at times hand to hand. At a pause in the action Will noticed across the street the Trading Post where in 1856, on the journey up from Tennessee, he had seen the giant Osage Indians and his father had bought the Colt revolver that was now warm in his hand. That had been only six years and a few months ago. He was a ten year old boy then. Now, he was a man, soon to be seventeen.

With dusk coming on, the Union forces, remarkably, were able to repel the final attack, forcing the Confederates to retreat to the south. The Union pursuit was half-hearted but Will and C.J. were chased by a few aggressive Union cavalrymen. Together they made their escape, charging up a steep, craggy escarpment, Will in front with Circus straining to make the grade. Just as they reached the top a single cannon shot exploded so close to them it nearly knocked Will from the saddle. It was all he could do to rein in Circus, who reared at the top the hill and pawed the air. Will looked down behind for C.J. and, through the smoke, saw that C.J.'s horse had taken the full force of the blow. Horse and rider had tumbled back down to the bottom. The horse lay dead with his flank torn open and C.J. was trapped beneath him.

The Yankees seemed not to have followed. Will guessed that the artillery shell had carried well beyond its intended range. Waiting to be sure he was in the clear, he turned Circus around to pick his way back down the rocky slope. When he swung down out of the saddle he feared C.J. was as dead as his horse, but as he bent down over him there was a moan and he could see C.J. was still breathing.

Night was coming on and C.J. was bleeding badly. Will dug frantically at the rocky scrabble to free him. When he grasped his leg to pull him out, it was hard to tell what was boot and what was flesh. The bottom of the boot was ripped away exposing a bloody foot. Will's mind spun in a frantic swirl. Drag him to a hiding place! Stop the bleeding! Get help! A nearby thicket met the first need. His own belt, with the buckle detached, became a tourniquet for C.J.'s upper thigh, but help, where was that to be found?

As night fell Will conjured up a daring plan, probably an insane plan. He rode quietly back toward the battlefield they had just escaped, found two dead Union men whose bodies had not yet been recovered, stripped off their jackets and collected both their caps. Back with C.J. every move to get him out of his grey and into blue brought a cry of pain. By the time Will was finished and exchanged his own jacket, he fell asleep exhausted.

Two hours later he woke with a start and, clearing his head, he worked out the rest of his plan. He lifted C.J.'s dead weight and stood him up against Circus, then summoning all his strength, he hefted him up across in front of the saddle. Now came the hard part. Moving slowly, he made his way back to where he hoped to find the Federals. Without knowing how close he came, he slipped by their pickets. When he was within fifty yards and could see their campfires and hear voices, he stopped and waited for dawn, patting Circus' neck to keep him quiet. He couldn't do anything about C.J.'s moans.

The morning light was just breaking through a heavy fog when Will gathered up all the courage and calm he could muster and rode slowly past some tethered horses into the midst of the Union tents. His hope was that he would be mistaken for the first back of a morning squad sent out to recover the dead and wounded.

Two men, bent over their fires brewing morning coffee, looked up indifferently. It was a sight they saw after every battle, fast becoming more routine than sad. Making it that far, Will turned Circus to the left side of the bivouac where he saw men coming and going from a cabin. The heavy blood stains on the apron of one of them meant that this was their makeshift field surgery. Nearly overwhelmed by the odds against him, Will heard his brother James' favorite expression in the back of his mind, "In for a penny, in for a pound." He dismounted in front of the cabin, struggled to pull C.J. over on his shoulder, stumbled inside and laid him on an empty table in front of a doctor. He spoke with what he hoped would sound like a clipped Yankee accent, "Right leg's pretty bad, Sir!"

The doctor bent over C.J. and immediately straightened back up fixing Will with a glare. There was C.J.'s brass C.S.A. buckle showing between the open edges of the Yankee jacket. The doctor pulled the jacket back to cover it, grabbed Will by the sleeve, dragged him to a corner of the room and spoke with soft anger, "What the blazes you think you're doin' Reb?"

Will said nothing but put his hand on the butt of his Colt and met the doctor's stare. They both were frozen in the moment, a more bizarre moment than either of them could grasp. The doctor's shoulders then drooped with the fatigue of his grim work, surrendering to the preposterous challenge. Looking into Will's steely blue eyes and seeing a mixture of fear and determination, he said, "Leave your pistol where it is, son. My job is to do no harm, to save lives if I can."

He spoke further, still softly but more gently with the enunciation of a cultured man. "In all my time so far in this insane fight, I haven't seen any blood yet that was either blue or grey. I have no idea whether I can save your friend's leg or even save his life, but trust me, son, I'll do my best."

"Now about-face, walk through that door in front of you, get on your horse and find your way back to wherever the hell you came from." And in a whisper he added, like he might have spoken to a mischievous child, "Skeedaddle!"

Trying to look casual Will tipped the bill of his Union cap down a bit, swung up on Circus, and wove his way back between the campfires and tents as the fog began to clear. When he was well into the woods past where any pickets might have been, he threw off the jacket that could have got him hanged, stifled a Rebel shout, put his spurs to Circus' flank and galloped off uncertain which way to go, hoping to get back to his brigade.

CHAPTER SIX

C.J.'s impact on Will's life only became clear after he had to leave him with the Yankee doctor outside of Springfield. The kinds of questions Will sometimes had were not the kind of questions his officers wanted to hear, most of all Colonel Shelby, who was always leaning forward into battle, confident the cause was just and the South would prevail.

C.J. was always open to questions and kept confidences. What troubled Will were the reports that filtered in about what was happening to people all around the state at the hands of guerilla bands, not just to Yankee sympathizers but also to families supporting the south. John Edwards, whom Will and C.J. met in camp the night before the battle of Wilson's Creek, had become Shelby's adjutant. He was full of praise for the non-regular rebel fighters, especially Quantrill. Will had heard him explain that a Yankee General issued

Order Number Two, a couple of months back, identifying all such rebel gangs, called "bushwhackers," as outlaws. They were to be executed when caught. Edwards explained that the Confederate Congress a few weeks later in April, 1862, passed the Partisan Rangers Act which gave legitimacy to guerilla rebel bands and made their leaders officers. Stories of their raids passed among the regulars, but it was not until a letter from Eliza reached him in early June that he learned how fierce the conflict between the Union forces and the Partisans had become.

"To Will Webb, Shelby's Brigade
May 19, 1863

Dearest Will,
     I'm rushing to scribble this to you. I don't know where you are and only pray you're still alive. I'm trusting this will get to Maebelle and she will see it gets sent on to you.
     These have been the most horrible two days of my life. Yesterday Tom Livingston and his men caught a group of Federals, mostly Negra soldiers, taking supplies from the Radar's place and killed most of them. Some of our neighbors went over after Livingston and his men rode off and found bloody beaten bodies everywhere. They were so upset about it they couldn't speak of the details.
     The rumors are that the farms of Jonathan Rusk and his son Reuben, southeast of us, have been burnt. Not certain whether it was yesterday or early this morning. Don't know for sure who did it. We heard that James Oliver, Reuben's young son, said it was bushwhackers. Everyone knows that, except for Jonathan's son David, who rides with

Livingston, his other four sons are fighting for the North. Mother grieves for them anyway. They've been good friends. I didn't know it before but when we heard the news about their farms she told me how Jonathan and Reuben put up a big bond in court to help with legal things when Daddy died.

The Union command is furious about what happened at the Radar farm to their men. They've taken over Sherwood and ordered people to leave the area. The word goin' around is that Sherwood and houses for five miles around are going to be burnt. Last night we packed what our ox wagon would hold and we're leaving today. I fear most all of our things will be burnt up with the house.

The world has gone mad, Will. Things used to be clear to me. Now whichever side you're on, it looks like the war will get you. Nothin' seems right or good anymore. So many have died and whether you're for the South or not, dead is dead. And it's not just soldiers, but women and children.

I wish I could write sweet things to you but there's no time and all this evil has pretty much burnt it out of me anyhow. I can't tell you where to find me. Mother just says somewhere down in Texas, where we'll be safe.
Your Eliza."

Unbeknownst to either Eliza or Will, that same day a long second letter was sent by another Eliza, Elizabeth Jane Rusk, to her older brother Wes.

"To Lt. William Wesley Rusk
Company C, 76th Missouri Regiment
May 17, 1863

Dear Wes:

I'm writing this from your father-in-law's place. They're puttin' me up till I can figure out what to do.

It's hard to know where to begin, so many horrible things are happenin' here. Last week we had a late supper and a young Union soldier had come over to visit. There was a loud banging at father's door and, not waitin' for anyone to answer, some Union militia men came crashing in with their guns drawn. "There he is," one of them shouted. "That's him, that's the rebel." Before any of us could say anythin' someone fired and hit our young visitor. He fell to the floor dead, right beside me.

Turns out the gang had word that David had left Livingston's band to come home for a couple of days, but they were mistaken and killed one of their own. You can imagine how furious Father was about such a bloody invasion of a Union family's home, and how scared the children were. The next mornin' we buried the young man in our orchard. We heard word that the man who fired the shot is going to be court-martialed.

May 19, 1863

It's two days later here, Wes. I hate to be the one writing this to you but someone has to. Father's farm has been burnt and Reuben's too. We're still trying to find out who did it but Reuben's son Oliver saw them and said they were bushwhackers. My heart breaks for them, they've lost everythin'. Reuben is off fightin' and doesn't even know it yet. Poor Eveline. She's got those seven children and nursin' baby Isaac. When some of us heard and rushed over to help, Eveline and the children had kept themselves warm through the night by huddlin' around the burning embers of their house. We helped them salvage what they could and pack their wagon. They've headed off up to Ft. Scott.

I can hardly find the words to tell you the rest—what happened down the road at the Radar farm. Some Yankee Negra soldiers were confiscatin' supplies from the Radar farm. They were inside the house and had left their guns outside. Tom Livingston's men caught them and slaughtered them. Our neighbor, next house west, went down after the fightin' stopped. What he described turned my stomach. The unarmed Negras had all been shot and then they were beaten and slashed. Parts of their bodies had been cut off.

We've heard it before, the fury of the folks who defend slavery and their white hot anger at the thought of Negras signin' up with the North, daring to take up arms. I can't imagine how it can get worse than yesterday, and just a ways down the road from us.

What distresses the whole family even more is that David is ridin' with Livingston and, God help us, could have been part of the burnin' and killin'. When this war's over, if it ever ends, how are we all ever going to live together again, even in our own families?

I'm prayin' every day God will keep you safe.
Elizabeth."

In his own way, Will, from back in the winter of 1862, had been growing more and more uneasy about what the war was doing to people across the state, both those defending the southern way of life and those determined to save the Union. After the Battle of Pea Ridge most of the

Confederates in Missouri like his brigade under Shelby, focused on interrupting Union supply lines and such local victories as they could manage. If the Generals truly believed the war could be won and that Missouri could be reclaimed for the South, the rank and file soldiers were less convinced and that was apparent in the growing number of them who dropped out and went home to their farms and families.

Where orders came from was often a puzzle, as were those that came in the autumn of 1863, September 22. Shelby stirred the cavalry brigade with a fiery speech and led them out of Arkansas again on a month long zig zag raid up through Missouri. Having little supply support from the Confederacy their uniforms were a hodge-podge of farm clothes, some Confederate grey and a lot of Union blue.

In the first skirmish with 200 Yankees at Neosho, they lost seven men. When weeks later they reached bottom land just south of the Missouri River, they were badly depleted. An overwhelming force of Union troops stopped them at Marshall and forced them to flee back to the south. Edwards, Shelby's adjutant, claimed that they had destroyed over a hundred million dollars of Yankee supplies, but he was given to great exaggeration.

By October 17, the brigade had made it back to Jasper County, battered and exhausted from three days riding south as hard as they could. The brigade camped on the Kendrick farm outside Carthage. A cavalry battalion, including Will, was sent in to occupy the town for the night. Will was back on familiar ground, less than fifteen miles away from the Webb land. He and a dozen other men headed for the Shirley family's inn and tavern in the center of town where they heard lively piano music wafting into the street. Myra

Maebelle Shirley's fingers were dancing over the keys. A roaring fire and the smell of food filled out the picture. It was like falling into the warmth and comfort of a familiar dream. Myra immediately picked Will out. "Willy," she shouted, and ran across the room to give him a big hug. Will knew the men saw his face flush but he couldn't be sure it was because of the little boy name or the embrace.

The Shirleys, devoted to the Southern cause, quickly called in food–hog belly, beans, fresh baked bread and hot cider, a heavenly contrast to scrounging for food on the run and going to sleep most nights hungry. For Will it was nearly as good as being back home.

Myra Maebelle sat across from Will. "My, oh my, Willy, haven't seen you since the day you enlisted. Seems like an eternity."

How could he deal with the "Willy" thing? "Every bit that long," Will said, "Everyone calls me 'Will' these days, if you please, Miss Shirley."

"Now don't you 'Miss Shirley' me," she replied in teasing chastisement, "You know it's Myra."

None of his fellow cavalrymen said anything, but he knew from their smirking glances at each other that they were thinking, "So it's just 'Myra' is it?" The second round of cider did its work and the talk of warrior deeds flowed around the table, but Will needed to get Myra aside. She might know where her friend Eliza had gone.

The crowd was demanding more music. When Myra conceded Will followed her to the piano and whispered, "Can you tell me about the Vivions, where in Texas they went?"

"You mean, can I tell you where Eliza went?" she teased, as she sat down at the piano. After several lively pieces she finished with a rousing rendition of "Dixie" which set off loud cidered-up cheering and foot stomping. He took Myra by the arm and moved her to the back of the tavern.

"I don't know where they went, Willy…Will," she said. Everyone's runnin' down to somewhere in Texas. Pa's layin' plans for us to leave soon. Says we're goin' to a place called 'Seyene,' east of Dallas. Hopes he kin set up another saloon there. When Eliza's neighbors brought me her letter last May to send on to you, they were guessin' that she and her mother might have gone down to where her grandpa Thacker went years ago. I don't know where that is. Can't tell you anythin' more, Will. Sorry."

Trying to hide his disappointment Will reached inside his jacket and pulled out several pages folded together with a string tied around them. He had written them in bits and pieces over a couple of weeks. "This is for my brother James. Do yuh think you kin get it to him?"

Myra smiled and slipped the pages into the front of her blouse. She knew he was enjoying the glimpse of her womanhood and teased him, "That's what I do these days, Willy…Will, and I'm gettin' pretty good at it." Will knew what she meant. She and Eliza had quite a reputation as two county daredevil girls, riding out at night to both Confederate regulars and guerilla bands with letters, military messages and information about Yankee troop movements.

Heading back to the battalion assembled near the town square, Will knew Myra wouldn't be able to resist opening his letter.

She would read:

"September 19, 1863
Arkadelphia
Dear James

I'll most likely be addin' to this over a week or so as I find a bit of time here and there. Word passed around today that we're gonna strike out on another cavalry raid back up through Missouri. A thousand or more of us. Don't know exactly where yet, but General Price wants Colonel Shelby to break up the Union supply lines. I reckon we'll hit their wagon trains and smaller depots wherever we can. Some think we might get all the way up to the Missouri River. At least I've got Circus. There may be as many of a thousand of us. It's a hell of a long way, a hard ride through a lot of hills and hollers.

October 3
South of Neosho

Making a quill pen is easy enough but findin' scraps of paper is hard and real ink is even more scarce. I'm usin' some ho-made stuff. One of the guys whipped up a big batch months ago. Says he dissolves half a pound of extract of logwood in five gallons of hot water and adds half a pound of somethin' called "bikromate potash." Ain't sure how to spell any of this. He strains it and stores it in whiskey bottles. Says to make it real black he adds a dram of carbonate of potassa, whatever that is.

We been raisin' hell since we rolled out of Arkansas, September 22. We're a strange looking bunch. The Confederate government by and large ain't supplyin' no uniforms and almost no weapons. We have to scrounge our own. Steal guns and bullets from Union supply wagons and depots or pick up what we can find from the battlefields. Those of us who've wore out our own clothes now have to piece things together. A lot of it comes from dead Yankees so it's hard sometimes in battle to tell who's who. When we started out on this raid we picked sumac sprigs and stuck them in our hat bands to keep from shootin' each other. Due to hit Neosho tomorrow. Gotta get some sleep.

October 6
North of Humansville

Attacked Neosho on the 4th. Only 150-200 Union militia there. They fell back into the town square and holed up in the courthouse. We let loose some artillery and they surrendered right quick. A few of our men were killed. One fell right beside me. No bullet with my name on it today. Some of the Union people talk of all the burnin' and pillagin' we're doing. Guess that's what we did to Bowers Mill this mornin'. Reckon you know it was a favorite meetin' place for the Union militia. Pretty much the same on up through the state. Greenfield, Stockton, Humansville. Any buildin' the Yanks could use for a fort we blew up or burnt.

Strange sights all along the way. People who heard what was happenin' south of them had piled up all their goods and furniture outside their houses, expectin' to be burnt down. The Yankees had already come through earlier and set fire to the southern families.

There's a bad chill in the air tonight. I'm up close to the fire keepin' warm and writin' by the light. When I ponder what's been done right across the countryside with cannon fire and torch, none of it makes much sense anymore. Some of the worst I've heard is what Quantrill and over four hundred of his men did a few weeks ago in August at Lawrence.

Killin' and burnin' out Kansas folks, with a never-you-mind what their loyalties were. Heard that they looted the town and killed over a hundred and fifty men and boys, then fled back across the Missouri line into Cass County. Disbanded then and evaporated into the brush.

Seems week by week, month by month, both sides are destroyin' the country in the name of savin' it.

October 7
On our way toward Marshall.

Today met four wagons of families heading east from Cass County with what they could gather up in a hurry. They told us how on August 25, just four days after the massacre at Lawrence, General Ewing, the Commander in that border area issued somethin' called Order Number 11. The whole civilian population from the north in Jackson County through Cass, Bates, and northern Vernon County were ordered to evacuate the area in fifteen days. Ewing's plan was to stop the violence and bloodshed by creatin' a large neutral zone.

It was heart-breakin', James, to hear their stories and what was happenin' to all their neighbors. They said the roads were filled with people hopin' to find safe havens. Most of their men were away fightin', so it was largely women, children and old men. Kansas Redlegs and Jayhawkers had stolen their buggies, their good wagons and their horses. Some led small ox wagons overflowing' with their goods. Most were walkin'.

Even before they could leave, many had to watch as their homes and barns were burnt. They told us some people were beginnin' to call it the "Burnt District." For miles around all they could see of their neighbor's places were charred chimneys which they said were called "Jennison's Tombstones," after the Kansan Colonel who directed much of the destruction.

Do you remember the two families we met up in Cass County back in '60 when we were up there lookin' at land, thinkin' the farmin' might be better further north? Believe one family was the 'Childresses' and the other went by the name of 'Dudley.' Good people. I fear they've been caught up in all that horror.

October 17
Carthage

Got a fat sheaf of pages now. One more quick scribble here from the Shirley's Tavern. The brigade's bivouacked nearby. I'm with a battalion that came in to occupy the town. Got our butts kicked bad up at Marshall, east of Kansas City. Lost lots of men. Even more wounded. Been runnin' from the Yankees for several days now, tryin' to get back across into Arkansas. So close to home but gotta keep goin' south. Hope this will find you.
Will

The battalion occupying Carthage was surprised at dawn by a Union cavalry attack under the command of General Ewing, who had issued infamous Order Number 11. Will escaped and made his way back to Shelby's Brigade outside Carthage. He was certain some of the men sent to occupy Carthage had been killed and others captured. Shelby sent five companies to hold back Ewing's forces. Cannon and rifle fire shook the town for over an hour before the Confederate rear guard raced off to join the main force retreating toward Arkansas. Carthage held the dubious distinction of being on July 5, 1861 the first battle of the Civil war, preceding the eastern battle of Bull Run. Now, the second Battle of Carthage joined an accumulating series of Confederate defeats.

There was no rest for Will back in Arkansas. Shelby's brigade set up camp along Richmond Creek in northwest Arkansas. They were joined there by a party of irregulars which included Frank James, Jesse James, and Cole Younger. All of them were seen by the Federals as among the worst rebel outlaws. Shelby had sent them off in pursuit of a Union detachment moving down the Fayette-Prairie Grove road. When they returned they discovered that a Union force had cornered Shelby and his command staff and was calling for them to surrender. Although the guerillas were badly out-numbered, they threw caution to the wind and stormed in on the Union force with such ferocity that they gave way, allowing Shelby and his staff and a contingent of men to escape. That night Will saw John Edwards, Shelby's adjutant, writing notes as he often did, and asked who was in the rebel's daring attack that saved their bacon.

"You met one of them two years ago, the night before Lyon attacked us at Wilson's Creek," Edwards said. "Remember the fellow who told us about his step-father bein' hung and his little brother beaten up by a Union gang looking for Quantril. Well, two of the men out in front on that wild charge today were Frank James and his younger brother, Jesse. He's about the same age as you."

Will replied, "Pretty wild bunch. Don't know whether they're brave or just foolhardy, but we're sure in their debt.

That guy Frank looked so sick that night at Wilson's Creek, I doubted if we'd ever see him again."

"He told me some months later that he had come down with the measles." explained Edwards. "Wasn't in the fight there. Wound up a prisoner in the Yankee hospital. He got paroled but didn't lay down his arms and go home. Good thing, otherwise we'd all be Yankee prisoners now. Probably been sent off to Camp Douglas, that hell hole prison up in Chicago." It was not the first time Will had heard Edwards extol the virtues of the rebel guerillas.

The handwriting on the wall of Missouri defeats was either not clear enough in 1864 for General Sterling Price or he stubbornly refused to even read what was written. After Shelby struck north the prior October, only to narrowly escape back into Arkansas, yet another major Confederate campaign was mounted to take Missouri. General Kirby Smith, the commander of the Trans-Mississippi Department, ordered Price to mount another invasion of Missouri. It was just what he had been waiting for. Price saw it as not just a major raid, but rather a full-scale campaign to win the entire state for the South. Of the three divisions, Shelby, now promoted to Brigadier General, led the first one. Will would be going back yet again on a Missouri invasion.

On September 19, Price struck out from Pocahontas, Arkansas, with over twelve thousand troops and a number of artillery pieces, but it was a pitiful assemblage–badly equipped and so poorly armed that many men didn't even have a weapon. A fierce battle at Pilot's Knob, south of St. Louis, and a clever Union retreat left Price with a devastating number of casualties and a meaningless victory.

To the northwest the weary Confederates, now numbering

less than nine thousand, were overwhelmed by over twenty thousand Federal troops at Westport near Kansas City under the command of General Curtis, who had handed the Army of the West its first major defeat in March of 1862. The demoralized Confederates were repeatedly hammered as they retreated south, moving down the eastern border of Kansas. Despite several courageous rear guard actions by Shelby's men, the ragged Confederates were driven further south. Crossing into Missouri they found that Carthage has suffered the final insult. Confederate guerillas had burned down the entire town. The snow and sleet of the last leg of their retreat added to their misery. Disease and desertion steadily diminished their numbers.

Will was once again back across the Arkansas line. His fatigue was beyond description and he pitied Circus, who had been though the hell of battle after battle. How he wished for the perspective and advice of C.J. Some big decisions lay before him and the answers would now have to come out of his own head. Before there was any time for him to develop a plan, the Union consolidated their control of northwest Arkansas and drove the diseased and ragged remains of the Confederate forces through more freezing winter weather down into Texas.

The winter of 1864 in northeast Texas was miserable. As spring approached Will grew steadily more conflicted. On April 4, the telegraph brought a message to the troops from the President of the Confederacy, Jefferson Davis. He had retreated from Richmond to Danville, Virginia, and was on the verge of leaving Danville to flee further south, but his message to the Army of the West was to fight on.

In his proclamation Davis said, "Relieved from the necessity of guarding cities...with our army free to move from point to point...nothing is now needed to render our triumph certain but our own unquenchable resolve. No peace will ever be made with the infamous invaders."

But moving from point to point for Will and many of his comrades was precisely the problem. They didn't want to be free to move from skirmish to skirmish, but rather free from any more trips into battle; free to go home. General Shelby had read President Davis' words standing in the back of an open wagon so all could hear him, then added his own comments. Each of his brigade's recent battles was described as a glorious victory. He concluded, pausing after each sentence for effect.

"Gentlemen, this is how the war should have been fought all along. It's precisely what we have been doin' since Pea Ridge with success upon success. We must never, never surrender!"

In April a tidal wave of events crashed in upon the nation like a horrendous spring tornado sweeping the people, warring armies, and the structures of society before it. The options that Will faced now were sharply defined by fate and the overwhelming power of the North. The Union army had won one major victory after another. On April 9, 1865, Robert E. Lee, Commander of the Confederate forces, surrounded and outnumbered six to one succumbed to the inevitable, rode to a small house at Appomattox, Virginia and surrendered his sword to General Ulysses S. Grant. Another wave even more powerful than the first crashed in upon the nation five days later. On April 14 a rabid secessionist actor,

John Wilkes Booth, shot President Lincoln at the Ford Theater in Washington, D.C. The President died the next morning, April 15.

The war was now over but the nation, in addition to the hundreds of thousands of soldiers and civilians who had died in four years of brutal warfare, had now lost the one man who might have helped it follow the guidance of its better angels. Will was caught up between the forces that longed for peace and those unwilling to surrender. Among the most belligerent of the latter was his own commander, General Jo Shelby.

What was left of Shelby's Brigade and regulars under the command of other Generals had gathered at Marshall in northeast Texas just west of Shreveport, Louisiana. Shelby's address to his men was also issued in printed form. In it, hoping to encourage his men, he said:

"Stand by the ship, boys, as long as there is one plank upon another...let us never surrender.... We will stand together, we will keep our organization, our arms, our discipline, our hatred of oppression, until one universal shout goes up from an admirin' eye, that this Missouri Calvary Division preferred exile to submission–death to dishonor."

The earlier news of Lincoln's death had erupted among the ragged remnant of the Army of the Tran-Mississippi with cheers and salvos of artillery. Shelby, who was more reflective, saw it as the act of a mad man, a heavy blow to the nation–the loss of a leader who would have been generous to the defeated South.

Soon the word had passed around that Shelby planned to take his forces and move into Mexico. To implement his plans Shelby called his men together and said three lines would be formed. One line was for those who wished to surrender, a second for those who wanted to just "fall out" and go home. As a third option, those who wished to follow Shelby to Mexico were told to "step three paces forward."

Will had been struggling mightily since hearing the powerful news of April. What might follow after a surrender was full of dark uncertainties. Going home was equally troubling. In the minds of his neighbors in Jasper County he would forever be a former slave-holder, a man who had killed to defend the South. Several in the Webb clan had been killed by Union gangs and it was not at all clear whether he could reclaim his share of the Webb farm land. Mentally muddled and still feeling the powerful tug of the Confederate command, Will took the three uncertain paces forward. He would join the adventure to Mexico and whatever the Confederates could construct there.

Shelby's plan was to march the long distance across the state from Marshall to San Antonio, where the various commands would join up and from there march on southwest across the Mexican border. Any promise of what lay there could not match the despair and fatigue that most of the men felt. Scores of the three-paces-forward men disappeared from each night's encampment and with each passing day of long hard marches through the hot Texas spring, Will was more and more tempted to join them. With San Antonio just a bit more than a day's ride away, Will's first clear thought broke through.

Going back to Missouri seemed impossible and going forward down into Mexico was to follow someone else's dream, but Will had his own dream and it had been a daily recurring dream for over three years. Eliza was in Texas. He knew not where, but she was the one thing in life he really wanted. He would find her. When the company set up camp for the night a few miles north of San Marcos, Will left Circus saddled, and when all the conversation among the men had died out, when everyone was asleep, he quietly pulled on his boots, now badly worn from three years in battle. Then he gathered his bedroll and his fiddle, crept through the tents to Circus and rode quietly off into the night. It seemed wisest to ride straight east. He judged he had ridden about fifteen miles when he saw the faint light of lamps in village houses ahead. He found a wooded area where he could not be easily seen from the trail, pulled the saddle off Circus and laid out his bedroll. That night was full of dreams of Eliza, a swirling mixture of her choosing him to escort her home, of racing with her through the dark of night, of the feel of her body as they lay together in the Vivion barn on the last night he saw her.

CHAPTER SEVEN

The territorial whistle of a cardinal sitting at the top of a tree above him woke Will on the first morning he had been a civilian since July, 1861. The bird had his seeds, he thought, or whatever cardinals eat, but he had nothing, not even a piece of hard tack. Not wanting to be identified as a deserter, he dug a hole and buried his ragged Confederate jacket, the only piece of clothing that said, "soldier."

Circus, a piece of rope tying him loosely to a tree nearby, had found some breakfast grass. Saddling up, Will headed in the direction of the light seen when he stopped for the night. At the edge of town a hand painted sign told him that he was entering Lockhart, Texas. With the thought that he might exchange some work for breakfast, Will rode up to one of the larger buildings on the dusty main street, a combined livery and blacksmith shop. He flipped Circus' reins over a hitching post, stretched himself to his full height, took off his hat and went inside.

An old man came from the back past the glowing forge, sized up Will with a quick glance and asked, "Help yuh, young man?"

"My name's Will. Last name Webb. Lost my ranch job over by Austin," he lied. "Hopin' I might find some work hereabouts." If the old man guessed he was a Confederate deserter nothing in his heavily lined face betrayed it.

"My name's Elton Harrison but everyone just calls me 'El.' What's your trade?"

"Been herdin' cattle." he lied again. "But I know a bit about shoein' horses and done a bit of iron work." The first was true, the second a stretch.

"Well, yuh just might be in luck," the old man replied, assessing the lean strength of the scrawny young man facing him. Will guessed the old man was well into his seventies. He was badly bent from years at the anvil, and his hands were scarred and gnarled.

"Been layin' plans to ease back a bit in life and pass the hard work on to somebody else. Reckon I could give you a try for a few days. See what stuff you're made of." The old man guessed from the burnt-out look of Will and how his shirt hung on him that he hadn't had a square meal in days. "Like to share my breakfast?"

"Sure would," Will answered, "And you won't go wrong with me. I been workin' as hard as a growed man since I was nine or ten."

Back of the forge there was a small room with an iron stove, on top of which a blue enameled coffee pot sat, curling up a powerful aroma. The old man gave Will the only chair in the room, pulled the small table over between them so he could sit on the edge of a rough looking bed. It appeared not to have been slept in for quite a while. The old man divided what would have been his breakfast—beef jerky, some dried out cheese and hard tack. A bit of honey for the hard tack went well with the coffee.

Will saw the old man look at his boots several times and was not surprised when he said, "First thing we better do is get the soles of those boots fixed. Looks like if you stepped on a hot coal it'd burn right through to your toes. Down the street, just past the general store, you'll find the cobbler. Narrow little shop. Name's Earl. Tell him you're workin' a bit for me and he'll let you pay him later."

The shop was truly narrow. One could have stood in the middle and almost reached the wall on each side. The cobbler, who looked like he wasn't much younger than the blacksmith, took Will's boots, shook his head and said, "Well ain't much sole left but they sure are long enough. Size fourteen?"

Will had never been sure. By the time he was thirteen he had just asked for the largest size there was. He stood in his stocking feet, his left big toe poking through a hole, and wondered what came next. The old cobbler took his time, enjoying Will's awkwardness, then reached under the counter, pulled out a pair of boots and said, "Big man got shot last week. Buried him in his stocking feet. Might fit yuh while I'm fixing yours."

They were tight but solved the problem that Will, still groggy from a short night's sleep, had not thought of when he handed his boots to the cobbler. Working in his stocking feet in a blacksmith shop was hard to imagine. When Will returned the blacksmith told him that if he wanted he could hang around and help a bit through the day, then sleep the night in the back. He said he had to take his wagon over to San Marcos for some supplies, but a man would be there in the morning to show him the ropes.

A sharp metallic sound brought Will upright on his bed. His reaction was to cannon fire, but as he cleared his head, he realized it was the sound of a hammer on an anvil. He pulled on his clothes, the too tight boots, and went out into the shop. Standing with his back to Will was a tall Negro man. Had to be even taller than Will, maybe by two or three inches. He was wearing a long sleeve cotton shirt, sleeves half rolled up, and overalls. Will could see his powerful biceps and forearms pulse with each blow.

Will shouted, "Boy!" There was no answer. Then louder right behind him, "Boy, can yuh tell me where the blacksmith is?" The Negro worker turned slowly around, holding the hammer in his right hand and a piece of white hot iron with tongs in the other. All through his life in Tennessee and on in Missouri Will had called all Negro men "Boy." It was a commonplace for white southern boys, decades younger than a man slave, to speak that way; but the man looking at him near the heat of the forge, before even saying a word, conveyed such dignity and self-respect that Will knew he would never again address this man as "Boy." He might never use the word that way again for any man. The two men stood wordless facing each other for longer than Will was comfortable, then the taller man said with authority, "I'm the blacksmith." Giving Will a moment to absorb it, he added, "Solomon Smith." The almost imperceptible smile that accompanied his name should have eased Will's mind a bit, but it didn't. He was trying to figure out what to do or say next when Solomon took pity. "We got a lot'a forgin' to do today, gotta keep the coals good'n hot." Will nodded agreement. Still uncertain what to do next, he picked up a large hammer from a tool bench beside him and tested its weight.

"You won't be needin' that just yet, and I reckon I'll need to know your name." Solomon said.

"My name's Webb. Will Webb." he replied, uncertain why he turned it around that way.

"Well Mr. Will Webb," Solomon said, with a rich baritone voice that hinted of a tease, "You'll be on bellows duty for a while."

In most blacksmith shops, from what Will had seen, the task of cranking the bellows to keep the forge at peak heat was usually the job of young boys. He had never taken orders from any Negro, but his choices that day were few. He could walk away and keep his pride in tact or he could become a "bellows boy," keep the job and hope to graduate soon to more fitting work.

What he first thought was an easy and mindless task turned out to be challenging. There was skill to learn. A belt connected the crank to the huge leather lung and a pipe ran from the mouth of the bellows to the forge. Every turn of the crank blew oxygen into the coals. Solomon explained that too much oxygen caused a gas explosion that would put out the flame. Coals had to be kept clear of the air hole in the center of the forge and there was art in knowing how to burn the wood down to coals and when to add the harder "blacksmith coal," which kept the fire from burning too fast or too hot.

When El returned late in the afternoon from San
Marcos, he nodded to Will back at the crank and spoke
briefly with Solomon. Looking back at Will he tossed a little
wave and left. With nothing more said, Will had the job. El
only appeared now and again to check on things, fewer and
fewer times as the weeks rolled past. Solomon, in a casual
and sometimes off-handed way, wanting not to seem too
much Will's teacher, taught him about all the tools in the
shop and how to use them properly. As the weeks passed
they developed into a smooth working team. A boy now
manned the bellows crank and Will was fast becoming a
real blacksmith.

Occasionally when they stopped to cool off, or for lunch,
Solomon talked about himself. Will learned in bits and pieces
that he came from the Benin tribe in Africa, a people with a
long history of metal working, especially bronze casting.
Solomon's artisan skills quickly set him apart from other
slaves when he arrived in South Carolina. It was awkward
for Will to ask about what the passage across the Atlantic was
like, and Solomon never volunteered anything. Little he said
or did reflected his earlier slave identity. By the time he was
forty, Solomon had earned and saved enough to buy his
freedom. He headed west with no particular plan in mind
and, much like Will, wound up in Lockhart. El, whom
Solomon always referred to as "Mister Harrison," helped
him improve his English and made it clear to his neighbors
and customers that Solomon was a man of great talent and
Lockhart was lucky he came their way.

Will grew steadily confident in his own work and began
saving, with the hope of one day owning his own shop. Four

years after Will arrived in Lockhart, when he was beginning to see his goal in sight, El took sick and before anyone could realize how serious it was, he died of pneumonia. He had never married and had no heirs. Will was astounded when the town's attorney called him in and informed him that El had left him the blacksmith shop. There was only one stipulation—that Solomon, now getting on in years himself, would have a job there for life and that should Will sell the business while Solomon was still living, a third of the proceeds would go to him.

From the day Will arrived in Lockhart he had asked everyone he thought might know, if they had heard of a Vivion family, mother and daughter, who came down from Missouri in 1863. When business was no more than Solomon could handle he rode out to nearby towns in search of any word about Eliza.

In the fall of 1867 a brisk "norther" swept down on Lockhart. The warmth of the forge was welcome. Behind him Will heard the sound of a rig drive up to the shop door. He turned to see a sorrel mare pulling a buckboard. In the back was a large wagon wheel. In two years Will had come to know most of the people for miles around Lockhart, but this was not a rig he had seen before. As he walked out to greet them the woman sitting on the iron-sprung seat beside a stocky built young man turned in his direction and he recognized her instantly. It was Eliza.

Will had not seen her for more than four years. All he had was a long letter she had written the night before she and her mother fled Sherwood for Texas. He had read it so many times, folding and unfolding it, that the creases were ready to tear. He had hoped when he broke off from Shelby's Brigade that he would be able to find her, but Texas was a vast state and his searching so far had been futile.

It was more than a surprise to see her drive up now, right out of the blue. Will was dumfounded and struggled to collect his wits. Instead of a Texas "Howdy," he blurted out, "Eliza!" Only seconds passed before he could conjure up something more to say, but it seemed like an eternity. Will gathered himself, dusted off his leather apron and took off his cap, holding it with both hands at his waist. To his first exclamation he added, as calmly as he could manage, "It's been a while, Ma'am." He pulled off his right glove and took her hand as she lifted her dress, slightly exposing a high-topped shoe, and stepped to the ground. Her husband came around the other side of the rig, smiled and said, "You two know each other?"

"Yes," Eliza answered, "from the war." Another awkward moment passed before she added, "Back in my Mizzoury spy girl days, on my first night out, I carried messages to the cavalry brigade of a Colonel Shelby. One of his officers insisted that I not ride back home alone. Mr. Webb here was drafted for the job and gallantly escorted me back to Sherwood. Rode his big black stallion." She turned to Will and said, "Didn't he have a white mark on his forehead, Willy?" His name got the emphasis and she had added back the "y" of his little boy's name, "Willy," the "y" she had taken from him so dramatically that first night.

Will nodded and replied formally, "Yes Ma'am. It was a circle." Both of them knew his name was "Circus."

Eliza had turned a quarter round back to her husband so Will couldn't see her face, but he felt sure that, in her flirting way, she was reminding him of what took place the night she changed his name. He didn't need reminding, but it was images of their second night that filled his mind in that moment. That night he was unambiguously "Will."

Switching back again she deliberately dropped the "y" and with a smile so faint it left room for him to wonder whether the same images were in her mind, Eliza asked, "Still got that big handsome horse, Will? What was his name?"

With a small stutter Will replied, "Cir...cus," then more firmly, "Circus. He's out back in the corral."

Although she kept her cool and had surely been teasing Will, Eliza was so surprised to see him that she had neglected to introduce her husband. Not waiting for her, he put out his hand and said, "I'm the husband, John, John Jameson. Which is it, 'Willy' or 'Will'?" He was unaware of the interplay.

Will pulled off his other glove, stuck both in his apron pocket and replied, "It's Will, Will Webb. Pleased to meet yuh." Hoping to disguise the fact that he was really seeing individuals and not a couple, he chose his words carefully. "Where'd you folks come from this mornin'?"

"Over east two days ride, Lavaca County," John replied. "My wife's grandfather, Thacker Vivion, came down here from Mizzoury back in the fifties to seek his fortune and when Eliza and her mother had to run from the war up there in sixty-three, it was the one place they knew."

John switched to why they'd come over to Lockhart, "I'd heard there was a good smithy here. Got a wagon wheel needs a new rim. Lookin' to buy a rifle at your general store and do some bankin' business."

Relieved that he could retreat into business matters, Will turned his attention to the wagon wheel, but when John had said the word, "husband," there was a fleeting moment when he wondered if Eliza had told him about all of her teenage adventures, in particular the night with him in the Vivion barn, the last time they saw each other. He stole a look at Eliza and imagined that she was reassuring him. Of all her daring wartime escapades, perhaps she had kept that one secret. At least John hadn't shown any hint of hostility when he learned of their wartime acquaintance and heard Will's name.

Will tried hard to keep his eyes off Eliza while unloading the wagon wheel and rolling it into the shop. She must be twenty now, he thought. She was so trim when he first met her, easily taken at night for a boy. But now she was a mature woman. More than that, she was unmistakably pregnant. Meeting her eyes again for an instant, he thought he saw the same warmth as on the last night they were together, but of course it had to be his imagination. She had gotten on with her life.

Later in the afternoon the Jamesons returned. John came into the shop to pay for the repair. Eliza stayed in the buckboard. Will helped him lift his wheel into the back of their buckboard, iron rim still warm from his work. As he passed Eliza she offered him her gloved hand, sealed their awkward reunion with a polite smile, but said nothing. There was no "goodbye" and the omission almost seemed deliberate. For his part, Will avoided the expression and the finality that went with it. The sorrel was given a "giddyup" and Mr. and Mrs. John Jameson rolled away down Main Street heading east. Will watched until they were out of sight and only their dust lingered, a small cloud on the horizon. For several years, without being fully aware of it, Will had been nurturing a dream, but now it was time to wake up. He picked up his hammer, pulled some hot iron out of the forge and began hammering it into nothing in particular. The only thing on his mind was an overwhelming sense of loss. All of the hopeful Eliza "might-have-been's" from the tumultuous days of the war were now "never-would-be's."

From the back of the shop Solomon had noticed that there was something different about how Will engaged the couple who needed their wagon wheel repaired and it was obvious that what Will was shaping on his anvil was pointless, but he had learned that there were times to speak with Will when he seemed troubled, and times to keep quiet.

July in Texas was the Devil's doing, especially if your work was at a forge in a blacksmith's shop and the summer of 1874 was worse than most. Will had stepped outside in hopes of catching a cooling breeze in the shade of the big oak tree next to his building. With his back to the tree and the breeze in his face, he pulled out his pocket knife and was whittling nothing in particular when he looked to the north and saw a rider coming in on a handsome dapple gray horse, not one he had seen before in town. He had turned back toward his shop door when he heard the rider shout from a few yards away, "Hey, Johnny Reb, wait up!" Expecting to have to put up with the nonsense of some Yankee come down to become a Texas cattleman, he started through the door when the rider spoke again, this time right behind him, "Smithy, do yuh think you could fix a shoe on an old soldier's horse?"

Will now recognized the voice and spun around, "C.J., Curtis 'Professor' Jackson! Well, I'll be damned. Yuh made it!" When he palmed C.J. off as Yankee cavalry to a Union field surgeon at Springfield on that bitter winter day in 1863, he feared his wounds were mortal. The images of that day flashed through his mind—the cannon blast, C.J.'s horse blown out from under him and his right leg a bloody mess.

C.J. swung down from his horse in an odd way. He pulled his right boot from the stirrup with his hand, slid his left boot from its stirrup, lifted his right leg up and over the saddle horn, then dropped to the ground taking his weight mostly on his left leg. That he still had two legs, Will thought was a miracle.

A backslapping embrace might have appealed to them both, but C.J. shook Will's hand in the unusual way he had done when they first met at Cowskin Prairie in early July, 1861. It was a firm grasp and a small waggle side to side. Even blindfolded he would have known it was C.J. No one else he ever knew shook hands that way.

Solomon had come outside to see what the shouting was about. Will said, "Solomon, I want you to meet an old Confederate buddy, Curtis Jackson. Everyone calls him C.J."

Will knew from their years together that Solomon had an uncanny talent for sizing up a man in an instant and he could tell by the way Solomon shook the stranger's hand that C.J. had passed muster, especially when he saw Solomon's small gesture at the end of the handshake—a very slight, almost imperceptible, bow of his head. His short gray hair was a dramatic contrast to his dark skin.

"Solomon's taught me everything I know," said Will, and C.J. could hear the affection and respect in his tone. The old man simply smiled.

"We were just gettin' ready to shut down for the day. You gotta come out and meet my wife, Samantha, and our girls," he added, not allowing C.J. a chance to decline.

Leaving Solomon to close up, Will saddled up and showed C.J. the way out to his cabin. It was a short ride out of Lockhart. C.J. recognized the white circle on the forehead of Will's horse and asked, "Your horse from the war? Circus, isn't it? Still a mighty handsome animal."

"Well, he's gettin' a bit long in the tooth," Will said, "Goin' on eighteen now, but still as frisky as a colt."

"My recollection of the last time I saw you is a bit fuzzy," C.J. said. It was the backside of you as you left me, frozen cold and leg blasted. There I was in the hands of a Yankee surgeon and surrounded by wounded Union soldiers. You had some balls, Will, puttin' us both in Union jackets, and ridin' up to their hospital tent. The doc who treated me told me about it before I was shipped out to prison in Chicago. Said he thought you were crazy. I don't remember much of earlier that day, just you and Circus takin' me in–brassy as hell." Then looking over at Circus, "Guess I owe you my life, old fella," and back at Will with a smile, "And you too, Yankee." That was the second time in his life he had been cast in that role. It chafed the first time and could have got him hung, but caused a chuckle now.

Will's girls always listened in the evening for their father's approach and ran out the cabin door as the two rode up but hesitated when they saw the stranger.

"And who's this?" C.J. said.

"Lilly," Will's oldest responded with composure that belied her four years.

"And your sister?" C.J. asked.

Annie, two years younger, had retreated back into the doorway and was peaking around from behind her mother's skirt.

"You've heard all my stories about C.J." Will said to Samantha, "Well, here he is alive, bless God. Came all the way from Massachusetts." C.J. had filled him in a bit about the intervening years on their ride out, but Will always mispronounced the name of the state with a "toosetts" rather than a "chusetts." "C.J., this is my wife, Samantha. Samantha, this is C.J., in the flesh."

Samantha stepped out of the doorway and offered her hand. "Call me 'Sam,' everybody else does. Will's been pained about you as long as I've known him, wonderin' if you survived." Looking down at her youngest she added, "This'un hidin' behind me is Annie. She's almost two but still a bit shy around strangers."

Inside she asked, "How'd you find us?"

"My folks live up west of Waco," C.J. answered. "When I came back down from the east this spring I heard from a wheelwright there that there was a tall young blacksmith down here in Lockhart. Said to come from Missouri and rode a black horse with a circle on his forehead. We knew a lot of people from the southwest corner of Missouri came down here after the war and had heard there were some Webbs from Missouri around Austin, so I thought, 'That might be Will Webb further south.' Worth a ride down to see."

Samantha served their best smoked ham with tomatoes and okra, fresh from the garden, and the finest coffee C.J. had tasted in years. Afterward he and Will loaded their pipes and sat by the fire as Samantha cleared up and readied the girls for bed.

There was so much to catch up on, Will and C.J. talked over each other at times, remembering the big battles, men from their company and their leader, Colonel JO Shelby. It turned out that Will's daring ruse at the Yankee field hospital didn't last long. The C.S.A. on C.J.'s belt buckle gave him away, but it wasn't noticed until after the surgeon tended to his leg. Soon afterward C.J. had been shipped north to a prison, Camp Douglas in Chicago.

Talking about his years in prison was always difficult for C.J. There are some things in life that defy description to anyone whose life, whatever the hardships, has been reasonably normal. Later he would wonder, as he always did, whether his story stretched credulity. He began, "I thought two winters in Massachusetts had taught me something about being cold, but Chicago was a horrible new lesson. When we were marched off the train that January, the wind sliced through us as fiercely as a battlefield sword, but that was a mild beginning. Inside the gates was another world. If Hell in the Bible had been frozen torture instead of fire, this would surely have been Hell."

"I had felt pretty sorry for myself, but when I hobbled into the prison on my makeshift hickory crutch, that quickly passed. Inside was a filthy stinkin' mess, worse than any hog waller you ever saw. Men were walkin' about in the icy muck, mostly barefoot, with hardly any clothes on their back–thousands of them. Some wore bags with holes cut out for their heads and arms."

"Near the gate was a frame some four or five feet off the ground supporting, like a sawhorse, a long split rail with its sharp edge up. A naked man was astride it with a bucket of sand tied to each foot. I later learned it was called "ridin' the Mule." Near it were other men being forced to stand barefoot in the snow, forbidden to move their feet on pain of a lashing. Next to them were men who had been forced to pull their pants down and sit in the snow. As we walked past, I could see next to them the imprint from other men's backsides, a frozen testimony to the pain they must have endured. I'd never before seen such sadism."

Another one of C.J.'s "college learnin' words" Will thought. In camp during the war, unable to censor his learning, his earlier nickname, "Professor" had somehow reappeared. Will, always curious, often asked later in a private moment what new words meant and he never felt C.J. talked down to him or made him feel inferior. Seemed more like one friend sharing special things with another.

C.J. continued, "Cholera and smallpox were epidemic and if that didn't getcha, it was a miracle anyone survived the cold. Those who had blankets had them taken away. My second winter, we reckoned over a thousand men died in four months. And if yuh didn't freeze to death, starving was close behind. When the rains came the latrines overflowed into the source of our drinking water. Rations yuh couldn't survive on were cut further as the number of prisoners doubled what the camp had been designed for. It was a great treat when they raised the barracks up to discourage tunneling escapes and we found nests of big gray rats. Made some great rat pies."

Samantha, who hadn't heard the bit about rats, had come over with more hot coffee and a serving of fresh baked peach cobbler. C.J. could tell his tales of the horrors of the camp were disturbing to her and decided to switch to something lighter.

"When the war ended and I was released from prison, I got on a train for Boston where I'd heard that they took good care of veterans," C.J. said, "and I hoped I could pick up my studyin' at Harvard." Beyond the medical community, the hatred for 'Rebs,' as you can imagine, was still strong," C.J. remembered, "But no one asked about my allegiance when I applied to continue my studies. They put me up in Stoughton Hall on the floor above where I lived before the war. Well, the story I'm gettin' to here came in a letter delivered to me there. I was amazed it found me. The address was just 'Curt Jackson, Harvid College, Massachusetts.'"

I knew right away it was from Samuel Taylor, a fellow prisoner at Camp Douglas because he always pronounced Harvard as though the second 'a' was an 'i'. The last time I saw him was when he was carried off to what passed for an infirmary in the prison. He claimed to be deadly ill and his doctor had announced for all to hear that it was the deadly small pox."

C.J. shifted to ease the discomfort of his right leg and Will remembered how horrible it looked when he last saw it. "Sam's letter," continued C.J., "told the amazing story of how he survived. He said he was tended to by a new young doctor who was shocked at the treatment of prisoners, especially the sick. He enlisted one of our fellow prisoners to help Sam escape. When the helper went to Sam's room at the doctor's instruction, he found that the 'patient' had recovered from his fake illness, but was sitting upright in a coffin with a sheet wrapped around him."

"Sam told him the plan, 'Dust some flour lightly on my hands and face, then fasten my coffin lid loosely with just three or four short nails. The coffin wagon is coming any minute so you'll have to hurry. Help them load me and take care nothing is stacked on top of me.'"

C.J. spun the tale on out, "When the wagon, which was driven by a old man who was skittish about dealing with dead bodies, cleared the prison gate and Sam judged he was well out of sight of the prison guards, he let out a long deep moan, banged open the coffin lid, sat up and wailed loudly with his best funereal voice, 'Resurrection Day is Here!'"

Samantha burst out laughing at the "resurrection" story, holding her belly with one hand. Will had noticed her from time to time lately checking to see if her stomach was showing any sign of change. She hoped in a few months to present him with the son she knew he longed for.

C.J. picked his story back up. "The driver didn't wait around for more words from the dead and, when he had run out of sight, Sam struggled out of the shroud, climbed down, brushed off the flour, and unhitched one of the horses. Hiding in the daytime and riding all through the nights, he made his way over three hundred miles north, up along the eastern edge of Wisconsin and crossed into safety in Canada at Sault St. Marie."

Lilly and Annie, as they often did, came running back for hugs and kisses all around. Little Annie even planted a quick kiss on C.J.'s cheek. As Samantha said her goodnights and took the girls back to bed, Will and C.J. savored their cobbler. They had talked for over two hours, but weren't near done.

Will spoke as C.J. finished his coffee, "The war sure scattered men far and wide. If Colonel Shelby had got his way, I'd be down in Mexico now, I reckon. I suspect you may have heard that he refused to surrender after Appomattox. Gathered up all of us who'd survived to that point and dragged us off south with him."

"His plan was to go down to Mexico, maybe set up some kinda new country there, and make himself a Grand Wizard or something. General Price and General Hindman and a group of junior officers had bought into the plan, but the rank and file were droppin' out all along the way south, especially those with homes in Arkansas and Texas."

Will continued, "The force was gettin' smaller by the day. When we camped about ten miles north of Gonzales, I made the decision I had been strugglin' with for several days. I left Circle saddled and when everyone was asleep, I slipped out of camp and headed north to put some distance between myself and our rag tag company. A twenty mile ride through the night brought me into southern Caldwell County. Outside of Lockart, I bedded down to get a bit of sleep before dawn."

"All I had was the clothes on my back, my Colt, my rifle, my violin and a pair of badly worn boots that had served me through the war." C.J. smiled remembering them as the "Thomas Jefferson boots."

Samantha's voice from the other room, "You men better stop jawin' and get some sleep," made them aware that it was nearly midnight.

Will stood and C.J., with more effort, got to his feet slowly. "You're back there in the girl's room," Will said. "They're up in the loft. They love it there."

Later Will took a candle in to C.J. in case he had to get up in the night. When he tapped lightly on the door and looked in C.J. was sitting on the side of the bed. The right leg of his long johns was cut off and sewn closed above his knee. Against the wall near the bed stood a contraption of leather, iron and wood. The top looked like a tiny leather woman's corset with rawhide laces.

"Sorry," said Will.

"No, it's O.K. Come on in," C.J. replied. "Yankee doctor chopped it off soon after you left me and another Yankee, Doc Childress, up at Harvard's Medical School, whipped up this contraption for me after the war."

The device stood nearly as high as C.J.'s waist. He pulled it over closer and explained, "This upper leather thigh part takes my body weight. The leg below is made of wood that's attached to a partially wooden foot. The boot's supposed to look like a normal boot. This long leather strap goes up over my shoulder under my shirt. Keeps the whole thing from slippin' off when I swing my leg."

He smiled and added, "Ain't too good for dancin' one of your jigs, but works pretty damned well otherwise."

Will was impressed at how well C.J. had adjusted to the gruesome effects of war and would have liked to talk to him about his own jitters and persistent nightmares, but it was late and C.J. had said he needed to ride back the next day.

The next morning after breakfast and enthusiastic goodbye kisses and hugs from both Lilly and little Annie, Will and C.J. went out to the barn where Circus and C.J.'s dapple had been bedded down the night before. C.J. cinched the saddle on, turned to Will and said, "Apart from just seeing your blue eyes and reddish hair again, I had a reason for searching you out." When C.J. took a slip of paper out of his shirt pocket, Will could see in his face that he had something serious to share.

"Come back to my 'quiet' place," Will said, "Let's sit. I made me a spot where I can get away from things and try to get my head together." In the back of the barn, behind the horse stalls, Will had arranged some bales of hay with horse blankets thrown over them—one to sit on and another to put up his feet. He slid the footstool bale over to C.J. and said, "I've also got a bottle I keep hid back in the corner there to help settle my mind when it goes ragged, but it's too early for a whiskey."

C.J. smiled agreement and said, "You know I always had misgivins about the war. When I signed up I thought I was followin' the lead of General Lee. I guess you know he was first offered the chance to lead the Union army, but felt duty bound to defend Virginia and the South."

"My parents weren't slave holders," C.J. continued, "But we were Texans and always had a sense of bein' a country unto ourselves. We probably should've listened to Sam Houston. He riled up everyone when he argued that it was insane to secede from the Union and predicted that the South couldn't and wouldn't win against the industrial might of the north. Given a couple hundred years of Southerners gettin' set in their ways maybe, as much as I hate to believe it, there was no avoidin' a violent resolution of the conflict."

"Well, to get to my point, I wanted to share something with you that happened just last month. "Up at Harvard," he explained, "they built a big splendid building in memory of men killed in the War. It's called Memorial Hall. Last month they had a grand dedication ceremony and the key speaker was a Union Veteran, Harvard Class of 1862, two years ahead of me. Name was Major General William Francis Bartlett."

"I knew by the way he walked on crutches to the podium in that great auditorium that he had been badly wounded in the war. Later I learned that he was hit by a sharpshooter at Yorktown early in the war and lost one leg above the knee, like me."

Will understood, "Damned S.O.B.s. They picked off more than one of the men in our company. You get hit right out of the blue. No warning."

C.J. unfolded his paper that was worn from use and continued, "Tale was that he was fitted with a wooden leg and went back into service as a Colonel in the 57th Massachusetts Volunteers. Got captured, spent the last months of the war in prison and was in very bad health when he was finally released."

Will imagined a big sophisticated crowd gathered for the event as C.J. described the scene, "It was a hot humid afternoon and there were several speakers before Major Bartlett. The war had clearly taken a terrible toll on him, but when he stood, settin' his crutches aside and began to speak with a deep baritone voice, a great silence swept over the audience. There was a sense in the air that this was an extraordinary moment."

"Repeatedly through the speech he was interrupted with applause. It was one of the best speeches I've ever heard, Will. Newspapers carried it all over New England and beyond throughout the country, I'm told. My father even read it down here in Texas."

C.J. then reached into his other shirt pocket and pulled out his spectacles. Will was surprised that he needed them at his age, but guessed it was the fate of men who did a lot of book readin.' Leaning to his left to catch better light coming in through the barn doors, he said, "I copied down the best part." Then he read the Major's words.

"I firmly believe that when the gallant men of Lee's army surrendered at Appomattox they followed the example of their heroic chief and, with their arms laid down forever, ended their disloyalty to the Union." Then, C.J. continued, he ended with a powerful challenge, "Take care, then, lest you repel, by injustice, or suspicion, or even by indifference, the returning love of men who now speak of the flag as 'our flag.'"

C.J. then took off his spectacles, folded the paper, put it back in his pocket and said, "With those final words the Major sat down and simultaneously the huge crowd burst out cheerin'. Everyone in the auditorium was on their feet."

C.J. explained that as word of the speech spread through the country, people both north and south heard him as speaking for the nation—that we now must once and for all put the war behind us, that in every part of the land we must set about healing our wounds and rebuilding our lives and our communities. He got slowly to his feet, straightened the bad leg with his right hand, started toward his horse and said, "I've heard some pretty bad tales but can only guess how vengeance has raged back in your home county in the aftermath of the war, even more than in many other places in the country. And for the folks like you in Missouri and Kansas, the violence and bloodshed started years before the war began elsewhere."

Will wished he could have persuaded C.J. to stay on few days. He would have liked to tell him about how the horrors of the war had hung on him all these years since it ended. C.J.'s insight and advice had always been a boon to him during their years together with Shelby. He held the dapple gray's bit as C.J. put his good left leg in the stirrup and swung his stiff right leg over the saddle. Will was never much good at saying goodbye and C.J. avoided the word too. His horse turned sideways to Will and C.J. said, "Maybe it's time you took your little family and went back to the Webb land in Missouri." He smiled then added, "Can't think of anyone better suited than you to beat swords into plowshares." Out on the road heading north C.J. waived his hand up high without looking around and knew that Will had waved back.

CHAPTER EIGHT

C.J.'s challenge was much on Will's mind in the following weeks. For Samantha it was an even more difficult decision than for him. All she knew of the world in her twenty-two years was Arkansas and Texas where her parents had moved when she was a little girl. Texas was also the birthplace of her daughters. Beyond that Will was concerned about her health. This pregnancy had proven more difficult than the first two and a wagon trip back up to Missouri would be a grueling journey even if she was not expecting–over 600 miles as the crow flies and they were not crows. He decided not to tell Samantha or the girls about the danger of marauding Indians, just yet.

For himself, it meant leaving the place that had given his life some stability after the war. In addition to the business reputation he had built with his routine smithy work, cattlemen throughout the county and beyond sought out his branding irons. Complicating the challenge of starting over in business back home was his uncertainty about how he would be received as a Confederate soldier and a member of a former slave holding family.

The patterns of life for Missourians on both sides of the conflict had been devastated. During the war Union neighbors of the Webbs like Jonathan Rusk and his family were very much in the minority and they paid the price for their loyalty. Jonathan, his son Wes and their kinsmen, Milton Stevenson and J.G.L. Carter, were sent to a Confederate prison in Arkansas, and later some of their property was burned by roving Confederate bands. Many Unionists from southwest Missouri fled to safe havens in Kansas and were slow to return after the war.

Will remembered that shortly after his parents died, the 1860 census registered over 6,800 residents in Jasper County. Carthage and Sherwood were thriving towns. It was hard now to believe the news that reached him of the post war population count in December, 1865. Only 30 residents could be found in the whole of Jasper County. The descriptions of the destruction in his sister Jane's letters were grim. She said you could count on one hand the number of dwellings in Carthage that had not been destroyed by cannon blasts or fire. The court house had been burned and the public square and streets were grown up in weeds. The town was inhabited mostly by deer and the wolves that preyed on them. Owls had built nests in the chimneys that marked where houses had once stood.

In the years immediately following the war there was a lot of "gettin' even" with those who, as it turned out, chose the wrong side. The blood that had been shed in cold-blooded killings by gangs on both sides was not easily forgotten.

Will's own family had been especially hard hit, first by fate and then by human hate. It began when both his parents had died of typhoid fever two years before the war began and, early in the war, his older sister Paulina's infant son was badly injured when the family was hassled by a Unionist gang. He died a few days later. That was followed a month later in July, 1861, by several devastating losses. A mix of Federals from Carthage and Kansas Cavalry shot Paulina's husband, Jabez "Tall" Hatcher, and threw his body over a fence. Near the Hatcher farm on Center Creek Jesse Terry, whose first wife was Will's sister Mary Anne, heard the horses coming and tried to protect his children and his second wife, Mary Ann Stevenson. Unarmed, he had put up his hands and walked away from his cabin saying, "Don't bother my family, boys!" His wife and daughter came out of the cabin just as they shot him and watched as they continued to fire after he fell. Some of the killers were men both women knew.

On the same day another of Will's brothers-in-law, James McBride, was killed by Unionists. His wife, Ann Elizabeth, became the third Webb clan widow in one day. When the news of all these deaths reached Will away at war, it was hard not to conclude that there was a deliberate plan in 1861 to eliminate the men of the extended Webb family. And it continued on into the following years. In 1862 his cousin, James B. Webb, was killed in a land dispute when the Federals were trying to drive Southern loyalists off their farms.

Will remembered his brother James' prophesy the day he enlisted, that war was not going to be some grand adventure—that men would fix him in their gun sights and try to kill him. Death belongs to battlefields, but his kinsmen were killed at home on their farms. Even those who, sick of war, quit and went home were not spared. Tom Webb, another cousin, and his son Austin, had ridden with Tom Livingston, the Confederate guerilla, whose band terrorized southwest Missouri for two years. They had made a lot of enemies, especially after the spring, 1863 massacre of Union Negroes at the Radar farm and the subsequent burning of a number of farms southeast of Sherwood, including the farms of Jonathan Rusk and his oldest son, Reuben.

After Livingston's death in a battle at Stockton, early in July, 1863, Tom and Austin Webb like many weary Confederates who saw the war slipping away from them, went home to their farm. They had helped Dave Rusk, who took over Livingston's band, to bring their dead and wounded home to Jasper County.

Less than a week after Livingston was killed, they were back on their land in Jasper County where a couple of the Livingston men had been buried. Tom, Austin and Erasmus, a younger son, were out working in their fields. A group of men came riding in hard from the east and caught Tom and Austin. Erasmus was working further north by himself. Tom's wife saw the men take her husband and son away to the southwest. From her hiding spot she recognized a number of the men as their neighbors.

Will had learned of this tragic day in a letter he received from his sister Jane more than a month after the event. Jane said that Erasmus, from a hiding place, also watched his father and brother being marched away. When dawn broke the next morning Erasmus and his mother followed the gang's trail through the brush and found a horrible scene.

Tom and Austin, their hands in their pockets, had been shot from behind. Jane, who was usually a bit squeamish, was shocked and angry enough to add in her letter the gory detail that most of Austin's head had been blown away. Although Will, like many veterans, didn't talk much about such family horrors or his own wartime experiences, from time to time it became necessary to share some of them with his young bride. Samantha was a gentle, loving spirit, quick to understand and forgive, but in the first two years of their marriage she was often frightened by Will's behavior and, although he didn't understand it all himself, he tried to explain. Before their marriage he had struggled through his dark and down moments alone, but now his bouts with anxiety, depression, and the troubled nights affected his wife. Sparing her some of the more gruesome details, Will tried unsuccessfully to explain how the war and the murderous rampages that swept through the Webb family had affected him.

He told Samantha how news of the first killings of his Webb relatives had reached him at the outset of the war, soon after he went down to Cowskin Prairie for training right after signing up. What began then did not end until Tom and Austin were murdered two years later in 1863.

Samantha and her family had been spared the worst of the war and, although it was necessary to help her understand the impact of the war on him, it grieved Will to corrupt her innocent mind with such terrible dark tales. She sobbed when he spoke of the infant's death and continued to cry through the rest of his account. He deliberately omitted mention of the letter he received back in 1862 from his Tennessee cousin, Jack Webb. Jack had written after the first four deaths because Jane said she wasn't going to write about the horror that followed when the Webbs retaliated.

Jack recounted how the Webb clan had formed a plan to send an unmistakable message to anyone given to further attacks on anyone in their family. A telegram to Overton County in Tennessee had brought him up to Missouri to join the surviving men in the Webb clan and a group of other men from the south. "An eye for an eye" was how Jack described in cold matter-of-fact detail what they did. The words and images were burned into Will's mind. He remembered Jack's exact words, "I won't put in writing here who of the Webbs was with me that day and I don't need to say here who our target was. You already know his name."

Then Jack had painted a graphic picture of the Webb revenge. "We caught the murderous S.O.B., tied his hands behind him, put him on his horse and took him out to where the road toward Carthage crosses Center Creek. Everyone knew there were wild hogs out there. We hung him up so his feet barely touched the ground and kept people away from the site. He survived for nearly two days till the hogs finished him off. We'll see now who wants to come on our farms, shoot our unarmed men and kill our babies."

Will had seen every kind of horror during the war, knew how brutal angry men could be, and had killed men himself, but he always wondered whether he could have taken part in that event. He knew how powerful family bonds can be and how easily the desire for vengeance can swamp whatever civility and humanity remains in times of war.

Will's thoughts about going home were filled with such images and he knew that, as is always the case, those on the winning side translate vengeance into retribution. His oldest brother, J.C., along with Dave Rusk and others, in the months after the war, faced legal action from war widows whose civil suits charged in great detail how they had wantonly murdered their husbands. J.G.L. Carter and Jonathan Rusk successfully sued Livingston's substantial estate for the losses they claimed they suffered because of him.

Had all that rancor and hostility faded away enough during his ten years in Lockhart that he could now go home to Missouri and live in peace there? C.J.'s encouragement had set him leaning in that direction and he trusted his old friend's judgment. What tipped the scales a few weeks later was the arrival of his older brother, James, from up north of him in McLennon County. He seldom heard from James those days, but here he came riding up to Will's blacksmith shop on a horse lathered up from a hard trip south. It was clear he brought some kind of important news.

"J.C.'s gone and done it!" he exclaimed as he swung exhausted from the saddle.

"Well, good mornin'!" Will said, then paused for effect and added, "Done what?"

"He's discovered lead," James replied as he sat down on a big log stump outside Will's shop. He pulled off one boot, rubbed a sore foot, then took a telegram out of his shirt pocket and handed it to Will. "This came down the wire yesterday from Jane. Telegraph man's son hustled it out to my place."

Will unfolded it and read, "J.C. HIT THOUSAND POUND CHUNK OF LEAD WHILE PLOWING. STOP. MORE WHERE THAT CAME FROM. STOP. LETTER TO FOLLOW. STOP. COME HOME. STOP. WEBB FAMILY RICH. STOP. JANE"

Will knew the "come home" was intended for him. James had built a new life in Texas and was prospering. He had remarried and his Texan wife, Sally Mary (Bartlett) Callaway had brought substantial land holdings to their union. Jane, a Webb cousin, had married Will's older brother, Ben. Like James he had fled the hostilities of Missouri for safety in Texas but he, Jane, and their children had moved back to Missouri a few years earlier. Jane was the strong nurturing spirit in the family and had taken care of Will's younger brother Eli after their parents died.

"How're the twins?' Will asked. Sally had given birth to twin girls in 1872.

"What do you mean, 'How're the twins?'", James responded with exasperation. "Yuh goin' home now or what?"

Will smiled enjoying the chance to go one up on his older brother. "Well, I won't stand on one leg waitin' for a share of lead wealth. We both know J.C. But, truth be told, I've been thinkin' about it for a few weeks now. Yuh gonna tell me about the twins?"

Not for a moment buying Will's casualness about the discovery of lead, James played along. "Well they're gettin' better about sleepin'. We started out with the girls in the same cradle. One would just get to sleep when the other would cry and wake her sister up. Back and forth that went on night after night. Poor Sally never got any good sleep."

That night out at the cabin, Samantha and the girls pressed more for details about the babies than about what discovering lead meant. James was off the next morning charged with sending a telegram back to Jane with the message "MAYBE IT'S TIME. STOP. WILL."

Jasper County and most of southern Missouri had been bathed in blood from well before the war began until far too long after it ended. In the hope that it had bled out in the decade since the end of the war, Will laid his plans to leave Texas. He didn't know what it would take to sell his cabin, farm, and blacksmith shop, but it helped that things were booming in and around Caldwell County. Years earlier a bad drought, which began before the war, had wiped out many farmers, some of whom were Civil War veterans returning home. But where no crops would grow, cattle could be raised.

A year after Will abandoned the Shelby adventure into Mexico and landed in Lockhart, things had started looking up. A local rancher, Thornton Chisholm, rounded up a herd of 1800 cattle, brought them to nearby Cardwell Flats and put together a drive up north to the nearest railhead in St. Joe, Missouri. A couple of years later, Colonel J.J. Meyers started a drive right out of Lockhart.

There were mixed feelings in town about the drives. For Will it churned up a lot of good business. He came to be known to cattlemen in the county and beyond for his branding irons and always had orders backed up for weeks. The problem with cattle was that they didn't always go where they were supposed to go. Not long after James' visit, Will was busy one morning working on making his wagon ship shape for the trip back to Missouri, when he heard a distant rumble over the roar of his forge. It grew louder and louder and when he looked out to see what it was, down the street poured a horrendous sea of long horn cattle. He slammed the doors shut and dropped the wooden bar into its iron brackets. The whole shop shook as the herd crashed through town.

When it seemed like there would be no end to the flood of steers, the last few finally straggled by. A thick cloud of dust still hung in the air when the town folk came out, despairing over their broken fences and the sad remains of their gardens. A couple of houses had been shoved part way off their foundations. The best estimates were that there had been five or six thousand head in the stampede. Will suspected, but was not inclined to say, that a lot of them were branded with his irons.

Will's farm sold quickly for a good price and the last piece of business before they could leave was wrapping up the sale of his blacksmith business. For a couple of weeks Emil Seeliger, who was a German immigrant and pronounced his name "Zeeliger," had been dickering with Will over a final price. Emil was the other blacksmith in town, known to be a good craftsman but a bit eccentric, always designing and whipping up some new contraption. Will's shop was larger and Seeliger had plans to expand his business in a new direction. What he had in mind, he wouldn't say.

When a deal was finally struck Will carried over the papers one evening after work to get Seeliger's signature. He found Emil in the back of his shop sitting on a stool at a large drawing table, totally absorbed in some plans he was sketching.

"New design for a buggy?" Will asked, looking over Seeliger's shoulder. Shielding his work with his body, he said, "Na," which in his English was the opposite for his 'Ja." Sometimes it came out "Nein."

Seeliger clearly didn't want to reveal what the plans were for, but after a pause so long Will wondered if he would say more, he added with his words falling in volume, "It's vor a horseless carriage." This was offered grudgingly in his typical gruff way and with his odd "R's."

"No horse? Pulled by oxen or what?" Will joked.

"Na," he said again even more gruffly than before, fixing Will with a chastising stare, reluctant to comment further. Will stood quietly until Emil's irritation passed a bit and the awkward moment obliged him to say something beyond one syllable.

"Ziz not pulled by anyzing," he said, "It vill push itzelf around." He could tell Will was mystified and, still reluctant but hoping to finally shut down his intrusive questions, Seeliger added, "It vill haff its own 'horse' inzide a box behind zee buggy zeat."

"And when you buy my shop, your're gonna set up a place to build this carriage with a horse stuffed into that little box?" Will asked, trying hard not to laugh at this man whom many in town unkindly thought lived near the border of crazy.

"Ja," Seeliger answered, totally unaware that anything he had said sounded preposterous. And that "Ja" was the conspicuous end to their conversation. Will headed back to his shop, glad to have the papers signed before any more insane thoughts caused Emil to change his mind.

Will had lived longer in Texas than any other place in his life after his childhood in Tennessee and the Texas friendships and family ties were strong. Selling their property was easier than he had expected. The hard part was parting with many things that had been part of the fabric of their life. Nothing large could be accommodated in their wagon so all their furniture, including a cradle he had made anticipating his first born, Lilly, was sold to friends and neighbors. His daughters couldn't understand why they had to leave their home and were especially disturbed when the toy wagon their father made for them was put up for sale in their household goods auction.

The Sauters, one of several German immigrant families in the county, lived on the next farm south and were always quick to lend a neighborly hand. They had no children of their own and Will's girls loved what they called "sleepin' over" at their house. They also loved Mrs. Sauter's fresh baked bread which, when the wind was right, could be smelled a couple hundred yards away at their house. And when they ran over Mrs. Sauter always had thick slices ready for them spread with fresh churned butter. For Will and Samantha the "sleep overs" occasionally allowed them the privacy that was hard to come by in their small cabin. One of those nights alone was most likely the reason that Samantha was well into her third pregnancy. After two miscarriages she had nearly lost hope, as had Will.

The Sauters had bought Will and Samantha's bed and kitchen table to insure they would have the basics for their last days before departing. Samantha had hated parting with the bed which was a wedding present from her parents. Will's special attachment was to the cabin itself. He had lived rough in it while building it and his hands had been over every inch of it. When Samantha accepted his proposal of marriage he doubled his efforts and presented it to her on her fifteenth birthday, a blazing hot summer day mid-July, 1868, five months after their marriage.

The September morning of their departure for Missouri, friends and relatives arrived early with food for a barbeque picnic. Some brought little mementos, knowing that there was scant room in their wagon for any extra things. The festive mood disguised the feeling everyone had, the recognition that they would probably never see one another again. Blissfully unaware of such harsh realities, the children laughed and played their games. Two older children were trying to teach Lilly how to roll an iron hoop, running alongside striking it with a piece of wood.

Later the children from all the families went swimming in a shallow part of the creek south of Will's cabin. He sat on the grassy bank to watch out for those who didn't swim well yet. The scene reminded him of a hot dusty afternoon early in the war when two groups of battle-hardened men became children again for half an hour. He and a dozen or more men had left camp to cool off in a large creek a half mile away. Everyone stripped out of their clothes and jumped in. From down river around a bend they heard the noise of another group of swimmers. When they came in sight, the other group's blue uniforms could be seen scattered on the far bank. Both groups froze in place, each considered fleeing to their guns, then naked and equally defenseless, they remarkably and spontaneously saw the humor of the moment. For a half hour or more they laughed and splashed each other in their accidental armistice. Having washed away some of the grime of battle and some of its animosities, each group knew they had to return to their roles. Looking back at each other now and then as they swam toward their respective banks and their soldier clothes, they dressed, gathered their weapons and returned to their camps. Will and his group decided not to report the incident to their officers and they thought it was reasonable to believe the Yankee men didn't either.

Toward the end of the afternoon Solomon, the one person Will most needed to say goodbye to, had not yet shown up. Will feared that he might have been reluctant to intrude on a family event, especially being aware that he would be the only Negro there. But he realized that he should have known better when, just as the sun was falling low in the sky, Will's aging blacksmith mentor came riding up on his sorrel mare. Solomon was unique among the Negroes in the county. He carried himself with great dignity and a self assurance that drew people's attention when he appeared in a gathering of any kind. He was tall, lean and muscular. His dark skin was amazingly wrinkle free in a way that, were it not for his silver gray hair, would have suggested an age decades younger than his actual years.

It was a moment when a simple handshake would have been adequate, but when Solomon dropped down from the mare, Will met him with outstretched arms and gave him a long hug, each patting the other at the same time on the back, as men in a hug feel the need to do. Will didn't notice the surprise on the faces of a few of his other guests and if he had, it wouldn't have mattered. Solomon had over the years become his best friend. His advice, though sparingly given, was always sound and his ability to read people quickly was uncanny. Will owed all his blacksmith skills to Solomon and, because some of them came from an ancient African tradition of metal working, it was know-how that he could not have learned from anyone else.

Will's first lesson, after graduating from the bellows crank, had been how to shoe a horse. Solomon taught him to speak softly to the animal to gain his trust as he loosened the nails from the old shoe and pulled them out with the pincers.

While the new shoe was heating in the forge, the hoof was pared. The most important part, Solomon had told him was to "foot" the shoe properly—measure it against the hoof and, back at the anvil, hammer it to fit. Then the nails were driven in, always down and outward. "If you hit the nerve," Solomon said, "he'll kick you over the barn!"

Later came the artisan's skill with iron. Will and Solomon remembered together how difficult it was for Will to figure out how to forge the "S" shapes and curled ends that Solomon used when making an elaborate wrought iron gate. Solomon chuckled, "I reckon there ain't as much call for branding irons up in Missouri, but maybe you can keep bread on the table making gates. All those folks you say are gettin' rich minin' lead will need some fancy gates." The most important thing, however, that Will had learned from Solomon was not just the skills of hammer and anvil and making elaborate shapes. Through their ten years together his old silver-haired friend had bequeathed him a set of values, attitudes about respect for the other man, for all other men. Taken as a whole, it was a philosophy of life.

Will's memory of Solomon would always turn on an image of him when he came out, unsolicited, to help him finish up the cabin for his new bride. Without his help Will would not have completed the work in time for Samantha's birthday. Solomon had been the only person bold enough to comment on the fact that Samantha was only fourteen when Will took her as his bride. When he shared the news of his proposal with Solomon, the old man smiled and said, "Yuh sure like to take 'em out of the cradle, Will. Yessuh, right outa the cradle!" He enjoyed teasing Will, but at the same time he knew that Will's need for love had not been well served by the tragedies in his family and the turmoil and separations that war caused. Volunteering to help with the cabin was his quiet way of giving his blessing to their union. Solomon had no children of his own and Will had become like a son to him. No record of his birth was ever available to him, but Solomon liked to say, "Three score and ten–maybe more." At that age and Will reaching twenty-nine just three weeks earlier, Solomon could even have been his grandfather.

Paired with the "right outa the cradle" line was Will's recollection of Solomon at work on the cabin. The day they finished was stifling hot and humid. Will had stopped for a cool drink and looked over at Solomon intent on shaping wooden hinges for the cabin door–a special design of his own. Solomon explained that it was an African tradition handed down from his ancestors–that the door of one's home should swing on living material, not cold iron.

Like Will, Solomon had stripped to the waist. His sweat drenched body glistened in the sun and was rippled with muscles much more defined than those of most white men. Will thought to himself, "If there are African gods, this must be what they look like."

Samantha excused herself from the other well-wishers, came running up, stood on tip toes and kissed Solomon warmly on the cheek. "Solomon," she said, "We were worried you might not come." Right behind were her girls. They had adopted Solomon as their grandpa. Before Samantha could say more, each took a hand and skipping along led him over to where the food was laid out. They bubbled with stories about everything that was happening and how they were going to a country far away where their Daddy used to live when Circus was just a baby horse.

As night drifted in on a warm wind, Will's neighbor couples and friends from town said their goodbyes and gathered their children to head home. Only Will, his family and Solomon remained. The old man bent down for the girls' hugs and Samantha unwilling to concede to a goodbye touched his hand, smiled through tears and turned to follow the girls toward the cabin.

Will and Solomon sat alone by the dying coals of the fire that had kept the party's coffee hot. It was rare for Solomon to offer anything more that a sentence or two of insights, but he knew it was the last time he would ever see Will.

Raking the coals with a long stick, he said. "I think you've discovered that any man who works with his hands is an honorable man, as good as any born high or rich and in whatever race. But work is not just something a man does, Will. It's how he tells the world who he is. If he settles for anything other than an excellent piece of work, he's betrayin' himself."

Solomon paused, thinking of his ancient roots, and continued. "My grandfather back in Africa taught me, as his father had taught him and as he taught his son, that when you take your hammer to hot iron you're not just forging the thing in hand. We're not just forging a horse shoe or a wagon part. We're forging our life. You shape the horse shoe and the horse shoe shapes you."

His natural reticence told him to stop, but Will had become like a son to him and it was now through him that whatever wisdom he had would survive. "You will pull many pieces of iron from the fire and take them to your anvil, Will, but you only get one chance at shaping your life."

There had been many painful partings in Will's life, but never had one seemed more like an amputation than just saying goodbye to a special friend. Neither Will nor Solomon could have easily described the moment, but each felt it. Solomon reached into the saddle bag on the left side of his horse and took out a worn cigar box. He opened it, pulled out something wrapped in a swath of crimson wool and laid the box up on his saddle. When he unfolded the wrapping Will recognized the object as a treasure that Solomon had shown him once before when explaining how to cast things in bronze. That had been after several years, when Will realized how the skills of metal working had been passed down through time from age to youth.

The two men stood facing each other in a manner that each would have thought was casual and comfortable, but an observer looking on from a distance would have seen something that looked more like a ceremony. The object was a splendid ceremonial bronze hammer. Its patina spoke of great age and the elaborate markings on it hinted of meaning lost in the voyage from freedom into bondage. Had it been able to speak, it would have depicted centuries of African artisans bequeathing their techniques to younger generations. Solomon took Will's hand and put the bronze in it. It was difficult for each man to look the other in the eye.

Will spoke first. "I can't take this, Solomon. I can't. It's your most treasured possession."

In his rich baritone voice Solomon responded with finality that smothered Will's objection, "You must take it. And someday I hope you can pass it on to a son who has learned from you to respect metal and the artistry needed to shape it. One day, before long, the fire in my forge is gonna go out and I need to know my hammer will be in good hands."

The moment was so overpowering that Will had exchanged goodbyes with Solomon and was watching him ride away before what had just happened came clearly into focus. Will wrapped the hammer in the crimson cloth, put it in the cigar box and walked back toward the cabin, wondering how he could explain the meaning of this gift to Samantha and his girls.

CHAPTER NINE

The worlds that lay far to the northeast were wonderful and mysterious lands for Will and Samantha's daughters, especially five-year-old Lilly. Her younger sister, Annie, hadn't figured it all out yet, but Lilly had formed a picture of Missouri. It was where her father had grown up and Circus was just a little colt. Far beyond Missouri and across a big ocean was another land that her grandfather said he had learned about from his grandfather's grandfather. It was called France and Lilly dreamed of also going there someday. Her grandfather had told her that the way her mother's family name sounded long ago back in France, was not "Sublett," but "Soo-blay." He didn't tell her why the family had to flee France and how hard life was for their Sublett ancestors when they landed in Virginia.

At first the trip north was a grand adventure for Lilly and Annie, but as the days on the trail turned into weeks, it was no longer fun. From the first night out, when they heard the howl of coyotes and feared they would be attacked in their sleep, things grew steadily worse. Will tried to shield them from the tales of marauding Comanche Indians that passed between the families they met on the trail, but when they played with the children of other families, it was too exciting to contain. Will took those dangers much more seriously than he let on, but his greatest concern was for Samantha who, in her fourth month of pregnancy, was struggling much more than she did with Lilly and Annie. The first weeks, when it was still hot on the trail north out of Texas, were especially hard for her, but by the time they finally crossed over into Missouri, she was suffering and Will feared she would lose the baby, whom they both hoped would be a boy.

Beyond the ruts of the wagon trail, life was less rocky and Samantha seemed to be growing stronger each day. It was a tonic for her to be caught up in making a new home for her family, and everyone in the Webb clan welcomed her like she had always been one of them. The early part of the winter of 1876 was severe, keeping Samantha inside most of the time but she was nearing her due date and the cabin was alive with anticipation. Will's sister-in-law Jane visited Samantha daily to be on hand to help with the birth. Upon arriving late afternoon on the eleventh of March, Jane found Samantha in great pain. She raced to Will's shop and sent him to get Doc Whitworth. From the barn, pushed there by Jane, Will listened to the sounds of Samantha's struggle on through that afternoon and night. He had fought sleep all night, but had just dozed off at sun up when he heard Doc speak to him as he came through the barn door. His face could not disguise the message he brought to Will.

"We've lost her, Will," he said, his whole body drooping in despair. "Nothin' we could do helped."

Overwhelmed by the words "lost her," Will at first did not hear the rest—that the baby survived, "You have a fine new daughter, Will. She's a beauty and healthy as can be."

The idea of a son had so dominated both his and Samantha's thoughts for months that it was not until he held the infant that he grasped the reality. Three daughters. But the larger reality would be much harder to grasp. His young sweet wife was gone and it now fell to him to be both father and mother to three girls. Two days later, he stood in the small cemetery that had been carved out of the Webb land soon after they arrived from Tennessee. Lilly and little Annie clung to him on either side, bundled up against the cold. The clicking sound of sleet hitting granite grave stones around him registered more with Will than the intonations of the minister. Just a few yards away was the double gravestone of his parents. It was not quite seventeen years ago that he woke from a typhoid coma to learn that the disease had taken both his father and his mother on the same day, but it felt like a distant time and another world. Samantha, he, and the girls had come back up to Missouri to start a new life in the midst of family and old friends, but her death, like an unexpected cannon shot, had exploded those dreams.

The wind was blowing again from the north two days after Samantha was buried. Will was glad to be inside working by the warmth of the forge. He heard a wagon pull up outside and when he opened the door a tall young Negro man had set the wagon brake, tied the reins to his mule around the brake lever and was climbing down from a wagon that had seen better days.

"Come on inside." Will said, "Warm yerself."

The young man wore a wool jacket that Will guessed was homemade out of some plaid horse blankets. It had a certain style about it, as did its owner, who held his hands open near the pot belly stove midway back in the shop for a couple minutes, then turned to Will and said, "I'm guessin' you don't remember me, Massuh Will." The last two words came from years of habit and surprised both men, but the sound of them dragged the past into the present.

"Granville?" Will said, then answering his own question, "You're Granville!"

Granville nodded slowly and both men hesitated, not knowing how all that was linked to the name of a slave boy carried forward, now that he was free. Through Will's mind flashed an image of Granville as a little boy, standing among the family's slaves singing a mournful song outside his parent's cabin the day they died. That snowy morning was much like the day of Samantha's burial earlier that week.

Granville, with the same cheery manner that Will remembered from their days in Tennessee, carried them forward, "Brought my plow up to see if'n you kin mend it. Me and my new wife Amanda are share-croppin' some land down by Neosho." He and Will went out together and carried the plow back into the shop. Will assured Granville that it was an easy fix and that he could get to it in a couple of days.

Before Granville arrived Will had been forging some iron hooks to hold up a sign for his new blacksmith barn. The building was two stories tall with three chimney stacks reaching high above a gabled roof. On the second level in front facing the street were two eight-pane windows situated like eyes over the large sliding mouth-like door below them. Earlier in the day Will had mounted a bracket high up at the right-hand edge of the building. The sign to be hung had come from his shop in Texas and hanging it was for Will a statement of who he was. In the center of the sign was a five point lone star. It spoke of his enduring sense of being a southerner and of the Texas pride he had brought back with him to Missouri.

Looking for a way to draw Granville into his new Missouri world, Will said, "If yuh got a minute, maybe you could lend a hand."

Outside, Will had Granville drive his wagon close to the front of the shop and lock his brake with the bed under where the sign would hang. With Will on a ladder and Granville next to him in the wagon, they lifted the sign up and hooked it into its bracket. Back on the ground they stood side by side and watched as the wind gave the sign a little christening swing.

"Got some coffee on inside, Granville," Will said, and together they went in and sat down at a rough bench that served both as a work table and for meals. Will poured coffee into a new enamel cup he had bought the day before and handed it to Granville. He raised his battered tin cup to Granville and said, "We make a purty good team."

Granville smiled and considered his response. It would not be a toast response, but rather the thing he came to tell Will that day if the right moment presented itself. He said, "Good as any two men with the same father."

The words hung there in the air between them. Will knew with certainty now what he had long suspected; it was the explanation of his mother's comment on the trail up from Tennessee when he had asked why some of the slaves were light-skinned. "It's complicated, Will," she had said dismissively.

"Your mother, Julia, told you?" Will asked, "And Harriet?" Granville nodded yes to both questions. Will's father Elijah had also fathered Granville's older sister.

Both men were aware that the import of Granville's revelation would not be absorbed by either of them that day or in the near future. Granville was the first to stand. "Better git m'self back home to Amanda," he said and asked, "How much you reckon it'll be to fix my plow?"

"Nothin." said Will, "Nothin' at all. It'd take a lot more'n that to square things with Julia, and with you and your sister." Granville smiled, tipped his hat and drove off. Both men knew there would be other conversations and each hoped they would go well. One day, Will thought, he might tell Granville about Solomon.

Spring broke with an abundance of early flowers and blossoming trees, but Will took little notice of it; in fact, he avoided cheery things. Jane took care of the girls and a wet nurse was found for the baby who, following Samantha's wishes, was named Alta. The familiarity of work routines got Will through the spring and, without any enthusiasm from him, the business grew and Webb City was growing around him. His older brother J.C., ambitious after he discovered lead in his field, had arranged for the town plot to be surveyed back in July, 1874, on part of the half section of land he had accumulated, and plans were developing for its incorporation before the end of 1876.

On a trip in to the hardware and general store to stock up on horseshoe nails and some iron stock, Will paused to look at a handsome rifle in the store window. A finger pushed between his shoulder blades and the person behind him said, "Remember the feel of that, Willy?"

He recognized the voice and spun around faking a draw of the pistol he wasn't wearing and said, "Wes Rusk, you old cuss. Ain't see you for years and, yeh, I know what you want me to conjure up." What Will remembered was a cold day late in 1862. His brigade was attacking some Union supply wagons near Sarcoxie when they heard a second contingent of Union forces coming in behind them. In the rush to escape, Will turned to look behind him and was caught by a low branch that knocked him off Circus. Dazed, and on his hands and knees, he felt the point of a sword in the center of his back. The Yankee said, "Git up and turn yerself around slowly, Johnny Reb." As he did the sword followed the turn of his body and ended up at his throat. His captor, surprised, said, "Willy Webb, is that you in that grimy Confederate uniform?"

It was Wes Rusk, whom Will had last seen the afternoon of the fifth of July, 1861 when, coming back from Carthage, he stopped at the Webb farm to share news of the battle. Then, they were friends and neighbors wondering about the coming conflict, now they were on opposite sides of a bloody war. Wes heard the sounds of more of his men coming from behind. "There's no time to talk. Get back on that black horse and high-tail it out'a here."

"It's been a long time, my gettin' around to a thank you," Will said.

Wes laughed. "Whole lot'a things left unsaid, Will. Best leave'em that way." He changed the subject, "Guess maybe you heard that Dave and I had a livery business together over west of Joplin. Didn't work out. I think he needs a more excitin' life. Thinks he might like to be a law man. For me, it's gonna be farmin.' Got a place over between Carterville and Carthage."

It didn't surprise Will that it hadn't worked out. What amazed him was that they even tried. If half of what was told around about Dave parting company with his four Union brothers and rampaging around the countryside with Tom Livingston's Confederate band, it was a wonder his family ever spoke to him again. Will would have liked to ask Wes if it was true that Dave was in the gang that burned down his brother Reuben's house, and his father Jonathan's house as well. But even more he wanted to ask him whether after the war he had persistent headaches, the jitters and night sweats and especially if he had recurring battlefield nightmares. Will wondered, as he and his Yankee friend headed down the street in opposite directions, whether it was different for veterans who had fought on the winning side, whether their sleep was righteously peaceful.

Will was about to climb up in his wagon when he saw the back of a young woman going in the dry goods store across the street. No, he thought, that couldn't be Eliza. She was still in Texas. Still, he could wander over to the store just to be sure. As he stepped through the door it was as though the young woman sensed he was there. She turned and oblivious to anyone else in the store she exclaimed, "Will!" then ran to him and threw her arms around his neck. Will blushed and didn't know what to do next. After all, she was a married woman and by now a mother.

Eliza led him outside to her mother's buggy where they talked for nearly an hour, or rather, Eliza did a lot of talking and Will a lot of listening. It was mostly not good news. On top of all the tragedies in her young life–losing her father when she was only eight, her brother killed in the war, their house near Sherwood burned down, the long escape down to Texas–now Will learned that her husband, John, had died suddenly a month ago just after they returned to Missouri.

Had they not been drawn together so powerfully during the war, had each unbeknownst to the other not dreamed through the war years that they would find one another, their shared tragedies alone would have been a strong sympathetic bond. In the weeks that followed they spent as much time as possible together, each quietly confident that fate had finally decided to smile on them. Without saying it in their early courting days, they both were certain they would marry; but they had loved their spouses and there needed to be a respectable period of mourning. Eliza's mother Julia saw what was happening and did everything to discourage them. Eliza had never told her mother about meeting Will on her courier rides or about the passion they shared the night of their second meeting. In Julia's mind Will Webb was just a poor relative of the wealthy founder of Webb City. Her daughter, if she ever married again, deserved better.

From that morning at the dry goods store though the summer and fall, they began by lovingly consoling one another and then week by week were caught up in their long dreamed-of romance. As 1876 drew to a close they were married in the parlor of the local Methodist preacher. It was December 18, close on nine months after Samantha died.

The marriage bed was everything they had dreamed of since their parting night during the war and Eliza quickly became pregnant, but merging their families was a challenge. Eliza's daughter, Mary, was ten and loved helping with Will's baby daughter, Alta. Eliza's son William, two years younger than Mary, quickly attached to Will and loved cranking the bellows for his new father's forge. Will's four-year-old, Annie, bonded immediately with Eliza but Lilly, now six, had stronger memories of her mother and didn't want Eliza to take her place.

No longer the burden-free teenagers of the war years, Will and Eliza now had four children together and a baby on the way. Will escaped to his shop, but Eliza was overwhelmed by the duties of motherhood. She could not imagine how she would manage when the fifth child arrived and, like Will, she came to her new life already badly battered by her first twenty-eight years.

It should have been a totally joyous event when in early September Eliza gave birth to Albert, the son Will had longed for, but their marriage was already in trouble. Will had hoped that Eliza's love would bring him peace, but his headaches and nightmares grew worse and his thrashing about at night was so violent that Eliza feared him and came to think he might be possessed. Will had unwittingly struck her more than once before in his nighttime flailings, but the blow that jolted Eliza awake on the morning of December 6 split their marriage in half. She left both their bed and their marriage when she pulled a woolen shawl around her shoulders and went into the cabin's main room. As she stoked the fire, the thoughts that had been growing stronger for weeks now took clear shape. She would file for a divorce, take her children and move in with her mother. When little Albert stirred in his cradle, she knew she would take him too.

There had been heated words on other such mornings, but Eliza was past words now and, although Will wouldn't discover her intent until days later it was clear that morning that their marriage was failing. That evening after work Will sought out the one person whose advice he valued, Doc Whitworth. Doc knew things about how war kept troubling men for years after they came home and helped Will understand that he was not alone among veterans with his sudden outbursts of temper, his nervousness in waking hours and his nighttime terrors, but Will feared Eliza was beyond hearing about any 'whys.' The 'whats' of life with Will and caring for his children had overwhelmed her and were now overwhelming their marriage.

The morning Eliza packed up to move in with her mother, baby Albert became the center of Will's focus. Eliza was surely his mother, he nursed at her breast; but it was only as the wagon rolled away that the full impact of Will's loss as a father hit him. His only son was gone!

Loss was not a thing unknown to Will, but now he was swept away by a torrent of losses. That afternoon when he took his daughters over to Ben and Jane's house where they would stay for a while, he was shocked to see how much more frail his brother had become. There was the unmistaken darkness of death in his eyes–another victim of the disease that destroyed men's lungs. When he left and Ben reached up for his hand, Will felt like he was being dragged down into the depths with him. Another surge of the undertow was yet to come.

Back at his barn, as he started to unhitch his mare from the buggy, he heard a wheezing sound from Circus' stall. It had been clear for days that Circus was dying, but now the great black horse lay on his side unable to stand. Circus was only a horse, but he was the horse of Will's life. They had met every challenge together. Then Will did what it was his duty to do. The Henry rifle not only ended Circus' suffering, its sound cracked the vessel of Will's life, shattering the meager hope that remained. Dragged under by despair, he slid down to the straw floor, swung the lever action that pumped another shell into the chamber and, holding the rifle butt against his feet he put the cold barrel under his chin.

"Will?" It was the voice of Doc Whitworth over at the blacksmith shop. Not finding him there he went over to the barn and shouted again, "Will?" It gave Will time to lean his rifle against the wall, gather himself, and come out face to face with Doc as he opened the barn door.

Trying to hide what had been about to happen, Will said, "Had to put Circus down." Doc instantly knew that it was a larger moment that than. It was in fact why he felt compelled to pay Will a visit that day.

He had seen the despair building in his blacksmith friend, and knowing that it was not uncommon for veterans to take their own lives, he was fearful for Will's well-being.

Will did not offer to take Doc in to see his horse and Doc knew instinctively that he should keep Will outside the barn. It felt odd for him to take Will by the arm when he led him over to the forge where they sat down at Will's rough work bench.

"Lost a horse of my own last week," he said to Will. Without giving Will a chance to speak, he added, "I'll git the men that did the burial over to tend to Circus tomorrow and you and I will take a break and go fishin.' It was a moment not to speak, not to make one's own decisions and Will rarely went fishing, but it was easy to nod agreement.

It was unusually warm for a December day and not a time many men went fishing, but catching fish was not really what Doc had in mind. He rolled up to Will's house at dawn bringing fishing tackle for two. By the time they reached Turkey Creek, the sun had conspired to make it a pleasant outing. Worms were slipped onto their hooks and both men's lines dropped into the water.

Doc was surprised when Will spoke first. It was clear that his mind was rummaging around in old memories. "Mother read the Bible to us when we were young'uns," he said. "Book of Job was always a puzzle to me. How a God who's supposed to love his children could land so much grief on one of his faithful servants is beyond me. Maybe Job wasn't a real person and it's just a story to teach some important lesson, but I'm a real man Doc, and I'm hurtin' real bad!"

Not sure how to respond, Doc said, "I've seen it happening, Will." Daring to get to the heart of things he added, "I know it can git so bad a man might want to just end it all." The words lay there between the two fishermen. Both knew why they were spoken, but neither knew what words should follow next.

Doc moved the thought forward. He said, "An old preacher of mine back in Tennessee told me once why a man should never take his own life." Will looked up from his fishing pole into Doc's eyes.

"It's a matter of worlds," Doc continued. "My preacher explained that no man lives by himself. He's part of a world and if he takes his own life he destroys that world—what it is now and what it ever would be.

No one has a right in solving his own problems to shatter a world, wreck the lives of those around him and all those far beyond."

Will looked back at his line in the water trying to absorb the thought. "We're all looking for meaning in life, Will," Doc said, "but I think it's not something we discover. It's something we create, a thing we shape with our own hands."

Not having a response, Will looked back up at Doc who thought he saw a little light in Will's eye that was not there when they started the day. For himself, Will was thinking of Solomon and what he said about work and life—how when a man forges something well he creates a piece of a world. In the years beyond his own life, when men use what he made, they are in touch with the past, both the creator and those who hold the object in the distant future live in a world larger than both of them.

The fishin' was done. Doc and Will carried their tackle back to the buggy and for the first time in weeks, a clear thought with a matching intent joined in Will's mind. He had a strong urge to get back to his shop and heat up some iron.

Eliza finally won her divorce, ending her short marriage to Will on a bitterly cold winter day, December 2, 1879. The explosion of mining in the county drove Will's business forward and him with it. With a German immigrant, Henry Schultz, he introduced a new boiler-flue welding process that resulted in substantial savings for the mining companies, allowing them to fully utilize their old flues. It was a blessing to be so busy that there was little time to fret about the past. Perhaps it was the demands of work, or what Doc Whitworth helped him understand or both, but Will's post-war torment slowly faded. Throughout 1880 and into the early months of 1881 Will was barely able to keep up with his blacksmith work and look after his three daughters. Lilly became a second mother to Alta and Annie found her way through the trials of being a middle child.

April triumphed over a cold March with unusually warm days and an explosion of forsythia and dogwood throughout the countryside. The last day of the month was as hot as a summer day.

Will stopped and went outside to haul up a bucket of water from the well next to the large oak on the south side of his shop. He put the bucket on the edge of the well, dipped up a drink of water, poured a second dipper-full over his head then sat down on the large millstone outside the double shop doors. Tired, with his head in his hands, he looked down at his heavily worn boots and thought that while they were badly worn, his spirits had been healing. Head still bowed and his hair dripping, Will was about to get up and return to the heat of his forge when a youthful bare foot stepped into the dust in front of him, toes nearly touching his right boot. Then the second bare foot moved up, toe to toe, just as close to his left boot.

Will looked up first wearily, then with interest, taking in the charming lines of the body attached to the feet. Pretty thin ankles showed beneath a long skirt. Above a narrow waist cinched with a wide belt, a well formed bosom filled a crisp white blouse. Looking on up, he met the dark eyes of a young woman, her face framed by long dark hair. It was one of those extraordinary unexpected moments that happen so rarely in life, but when they do, fall outside the mundane flow of a day's events and shape all the surrounding moments.

The barefoot girl spoke before Will could gather his bearings and think of something to say, "I'd rather go barefoot, Mr. Will Webb, than wear anything as ugly and worn out as those old boots."

Will was caught off guard, not only by the gratuitous assessment of his boots, but also that this young woman had called him by name. Collecting himself he said, "I'm afraid my old battered boots don't know your purty feet, Miss. Never been properly introduced."

"You know me. I'm Alice," she said, holding out her hand with mock formality, "Alice Ball."

Will could not have imagined the conversation that took place in the Ball home earlier that April. Alice was finishing school and would turn 18 the end of May. Her father, Fantley Ball, was an aggressive businessman who had grown wealthy with his mining company. He saw himself in his daughter's temperament and often joked that Alice's approach to life was to "take the bull by the horns," but what Alice announced after dinner that spring evening came as a total surprise both to him and Alice's mother, Emily.

To finish his meal as he always did, Fantley poured some white syrup out on his plate and with his table knife slowly and methodically mixed butter into it. He spread most of the mixture on a piece of bread and carefully swiped up the rest in circular motions around his plate until it was almost as clean as before the meal.

"I'm gonna get married," Alice said, not bothering to ease into it.

Fantley nearly choked on his syrup bread and Emily cried out with a question that carried its own rebuke. "You're gonna what?"

"Get married," Alice calmly repeated.

Emily was searching for the next thing to say when Fantley asked, "To whom?"

"Will Webb," replied Alice.

Emily was not going to entertain any such idea. Her question was sardonic, "And does Mr. Webb know this yet?"

"Not yet, but he will soon," Alice said.

Fantley was trying to gather some calm. He asked, "You mean Will Webb, the blacksmith?"

For more than two hours Alice's parents explained, in ways sometimes constrained and sometimes explosive, why such a marriage could not happen, why it would not happen. "Mr. Webb," as they chose to call him, underscoring his age, had to be nearly twenty years older than Alice, who was born two years after Will went off to war. There was not only the age difference; he had already been married twice. There were rumors, they argued, that he had a taste for young girls. They had heard that his Texas wife, Samantha, was only fourteen when he married her. She was still very young when she died giving birth to their third daughter. And then there was the question of why Eliza, his second wife, left him shortly after their first anniversary taking his only son with her. The talk around town was that the war had left him mentally scarred.

As often with the newly rich, the Balls had a keen sense of their station in the community. They knew, of course, that Will's older brother, John C. Webb, who had laid out Webb City on his own land, was one of the richest and most prominent men in the county. But it was apparent that, for whatever reason, Will had not shared in the ore riches discovered on Webb family property. By the time he came back from exile in Texas, the wealth had apparently been consolidated in J.C.'s hands. Will might be hardworking, but he would never be more than a humble blacksmith.

"Have you any idea what it would be like to raise his three daughters," Emily asked. "Why you're only a few years older than his oldest, Lilly."

It was not really a question, so Alice didn't answer, nor was she concerned when her father said that he had heard that Lilly was not happy that her father had replaced her mother Samantha with a new wife.

It was unspoken, but keenly recognized by Alice and her parents, that the pool of eligible husbands in their part of the county left everything to be desired. The burgeoning lead and zinc mines of Webb City and the surrounding area had flooded the countryside with a host of rough and ready men whose main interests were drinking, gambling, and loose women. Some of them worked for Fantley. Beyond that, the problem was a brutal one of numbers. The war had killed or badly maimed an entire generation of potential husbands and to Alice the boys in her class, too young to have gone off to war, were still children. Surely, her parents argued, there would be someone more promising than Will Webb and what was her hurry to get married anyway?

Alice was unsure when she first was attracted to Will. It may have been when she was nearly fifteen and her parent's surrey had thrown a wheel on their way to church. Will had happened by on a big black horse and offered to take Alice behind him on to church and come back in his buggy to pick up her parents. The event lingered in Alice's mind for weeks. Many nights she had slipped off to sleep recalling how he had said, "Hold tight, Miss," and how it felt to put her arms around his waist. Perhaps it was his reddish hair and blue eyes. It could have been how he looked on the fourth of July when he dared to wear a Confederate uniform to the festivities. Or maybe it was just one of those things that was meant to be.

Mother, father, and daughter finally ran out of energy for the conflict. The parents were confident that by the next morning their view of things would be shared by Alice when she had time to come to her senses. Alice, lying in her bed down the hall, was thinking about how she would approach the humble blacksmith, Will Webb, and set the wheels of fate in motion. She knew that she had not been able to share her feelings with her parents, and even had they been sympathetic, she saw it as fundamentally not a matter of reasons for or against. As she drifted off to sleep exhausted by the confrontation with her parents , she remembered what one of her teachers had shared early in the school year, quoting from some ancient philosopher. It resonated with her and was imprinted in her mind, "The heart has its reasons that reason knows not of."

"You're Fantley Ball's daughter?" Will asked, "The little dark-haired girl I gave a ride to church some three or four years ago?" He wiped his hands on his pants and gave hers a feeble handshake.

"Well, Fantley's my daddy and my hair's dark, but I'm not a little girl now." It was less an assertion than a question for Will to answer, but he passed on the challenge involved and let it stand as a statement of fact. Will was taken aback by Alice's mature demeanor and cool self-confidence. Her implied question was a woman's question. Young girls, in his experience, did not speak so forcefully and directly to an older man. Will had always been a man of few words, but this was different. It seemed like an eternity before a response came to mind. He had the odd feeling of being suddenly jerked back into his pre-war adolescence, to the humbling shyness of his boyhood. Alice waited, having laid down the challenge. Finally from somewhere Will's inept response rose to the surface, "Reckon your hair's a fair bit longer now."

Alice smiled at his awkwardness. She was clearly in control of the moment. She held out her heel-less right high button shoe to Will, took her left shoe from under her left arm and stood it up on the millstone where he had been sitting. Then she reached into her skirt pocket and held up the detached heel. "Blacksmith Webb," she asked, continuing her tease, "Can you repair my shoe? The heel's kinda come off."

Will was still flummoxed and trying to gather his wits so Alice reached down, took his hand, put her right shoe in it and then put in his other hand the heel that had broken off. It was a great relief for things to turn practical and for Will to look away from her eyes to the heel. Practicality had in many difficult moments in life been a useful haven. In this moment, it allowed him to escape from the corner this teenage girl had backed him into. He turned back into his shop where he could be in command. In the world of his work, he expected to speak more easily. There he had a shoemaker's iron last mounted on a cross cut section of a tree trunk. "I'm not much of a cobbler, Miss Ball," he said, gathering his bearings, but inadvertently by the slight intimacy of using her name, he slipped back into something beyond pure business. "Back in the war, I did a bit of emergency boot repair, when we were not being shot at," he added, but the small humor he intended fell flat and his last four words trailed off as he turned to search for some boot nails.

Will's back was to Alice, but he felt her dark eyes on him as he spread the top of her shoe open on the iron last, arranged the heel beneath it and drove in four small nails. Not letting him escape she moved around beside him as he flipped the shoe over, fitted it on the iron last and gently hammered the bottom of the heel, setting the nail heads in deep. He then tapped the heel from the bottom for good measure and carefully cut two thin pieces of leather for the heel insoles.

Alice bent over to watch him shaping the inserts with his sharp knife. Her bosom brushed against his arm so lightly that Will was unsure if it had really happened. He removed the heel insert from her good shoe, smeared some leather harness glue on both pieces, slipped one into each shoe, then pressed them firmly in place. The shoes were dainty in his rough hands as he held the pair together, toes facing him, and handed them back to Alice. In his mind the two insoles were a step beyond what she might have expected, especially matching the insert in the repaired shoe with another in the good shoe. It was something Solomon had taught him in the early days of his apprenticeship—always do a bit more than your customer expects you to do and never charge extra for it.

When Alice had moved uncomfortably close to him, a girl he judged had to be sixteen or seventeen years younger than he, he had caught a hint of her perfume over the coarse scent of horses, burning coals and hot iron. He couldn't help but wonder for a fleeting second whether or not the heel had come loose of its own accord, but that thought was quickly swept away by her cheery, but jokingly formal response, "Thank you very much, Mr. Blacksmith Webb." She did not ask him what she owed, nor had he thought about it. Their moment was well outside the realm of craftsman and customer. Whatever the strange thing was that happened between them in this high button shoe exchange, it clearly had nothing to do with money.

There was something almost sprite-like about the way Alice spun around at the shop door, her skirt swirling around her ankles. Offering no further comment she skipped across the dirt road in front of Will's shop and danced down the grassy slope, heading east in the direction of her parent's large home. Unlike the sturdy gait of a man and of many older women, she put one foot directly in front of the other and seemed almost to be floating on a sliver of air above the grass. Still barefoot she held one shoe by its top in each hand, left shoe in her left hand, right shoe in her right. Why it mattered he did not know, but Will tried without success to remember whether it was the right or the left he had repaired.

The total time of the cobbler transaction between them had been just a few minutes, but for Will everything else about the day receded into insignificance as he watched her depart. Not turning around, but confident he was still watching her and in answer to his unspoken question, she raised her right arm and gaily waved her hand over her head waggling her right shoe.

Will was very glad his partner Schultz was not in that day and especially grateful that none his daughters were there, hanging around to watch him work as they often did. Young Miss Ball had broken into his day unexpectedly, but deliberately, and in a scant few moments had spun everything in his life around. He had a strange sensation, one he had never experienced before in life–that this young woman, Alice Ball the thief, had stolen something from him and he didn't mind. William James Webb–soldier, blacksmith, father, survivor– didn't mind. He really didn't mind at all.

EPILOGUE

On October 8, 1881, a year and a half after Will repaired Alice's high button shoe, they were joined in marriage. Alice had just turned eighteen the previous May and Will was thirty-five. What she stole from Will that spring day in 1880 was returned many times over in the next thirty-nine years. With her bright, cheery spirit Alice quickly won over Will's three daughters and the following summer she gave birth to Alonzo. In the next ten years four more sons followed: William Fantley, Earl Japhis, George and Jim. Few men in the county were taller or more handsome than William James Webb's five grown sons. Alice brought to Will the happiness and peace that had long eluded him and their married life together was longer than the lives of many nineteenth century men. Will was eighty-four when he died in 1930 and, although she was seventeen years younger than he, Alice took her place beside him eighteen months later at the top of a hill in the Webb City Cemetery.

John C. Webb, Will's older brother who laid out the town of Webb City on his own land, died in 1883 only nine years after the discovery of lead ore on his land made him a wealthy man. The results of a post war civil suit by Union widows charging him with the murder of their husbands is lost to history and apparently did not linger to tarnish his reputation as Webb City's founder.

Eliza's life, like Will's, had been a series of tragedies: the accidental death of her father when she was only eight, her brother lost in the war, the family home burned, exile in Texas, her husband's death after they returned to Missouri, and the failure of her marriage to Will. Only one month after her divorce became final one last family tragedy struck. Her first son, William Jameson, died a few months before his tenth birthday. Eliza reverted to her first husband's name, "Jameson," and never remarried. She lived out her life with her mother Julia, who died at age eighty-two. Mining on the Vivion land generated wealth for the family and in later life Eliza was happy to have her youthful Confederate adventures forgotten.

Albert Webb, the son of Eliza and Will Webb's ill-fated marriage inherited the talent for making things from his father and some of the adventurous spirit of his mother. After several successful years in mining, he established a livery business in an impressive new building in Webb City. Like his father he loved horses but unlike his father he was an early automobile enthusiast and quickly made the transition to an "automobile livery." Early on he was a bicycle racer and later became an auto racer, defeating the famous

Barney Oldfield to win the dirt track trophy race at the 1904 St. Louis World Fair.

He is credited with inventing the first automobile powered fire engine pumper which was manufactured in Missouri, Indiana, and Pennsylvania and sold internationally. During World War I he was in charge of tank production in Cleveland, Ohio, and after the war worked with Eddie Rickenbacker in his new motorcar company. In collaboration with another automobile manufacturing giant, Carl Fisher, Albert built the land clearing equipment Fisher's company used in developing Miami Beach.

Jonathan Rusk, the patriarch of the Rusks in southwest Missouri, had moved his family there from Indiana in 1838. He traded a horse and one hundred dollars for his first piece of land. By 1861 he had acquired several hundred acres. By the time of his death he had accumulated over twelve hundred acres. Jonathan survived imprisonment in Arkansas during the war but his health was never the same afterward. Shortly after the war he successfully sued the estate of the Confederate Tom Livingston, receiving $2300 for wartime losses on his farm. Jonathan lived to see his Confederate son, David, reconciled with the family and watched his second family grow along with his land holdings and cattle stock.

The result of civil suits brought against David Rusk along with Johh C. Webb and other former Confederates shortly after the war by widows from Union families is also unknown. After failing in a post-war livery business venture in Joplin with his older Union brother, William Wesley Rusk (against whom he had fought in Missouri skirmishes) David put aside his hostile attitude toward the federal government and found the postwar gun-toting excitement he needed by becoming a U.S. Marshall.

Like a number of other infamous former Confederate guerillas Jesse James and his brother Frank, carrying the violence of the war into the postwar years, became outlaws, bank robbers and killers. Almost single-handedly John N. Edwards, more fantasist and fabricator than historian, created the myth of the noble guerilla. Edwards, who rode in the same Shelby brigade as Will Webb, became a Kansas City newsman after the war and used his pen with great flourish. Among his mythical cast of heroic former Confederate guerillas the most prominent was Jesse James, the so-called Robin Hood of Missouri. Such myths, however, were survival lies. They were justificatory masks that allowed their wearers like James to look in the mirror and not see the postwar reality of their violent lives. In 1882 Jesse, only thirty-four, was shot in the back by a member of his own gang to collect the $10,000 price that Thomas Crittenden, the governor of Missouri, had put on his head. His brother Frank, who surrendered to the governor a few months later, was tried twice and acquitted. He lived out his life on the James family farm and died in 1915 at age seventy-two.

Myra Maebelle Shirley, daughter of the Carthage, Missouri inn keeper and tavern owner, John Shirley, fled to Texas with her parents during the war. Like young Eliza Vivion she had been a teenage courier to Confederate troops in southwest Missouri. Because of her association with a number of notorious outlaws in Texas and Oklahoma and several marriages to robbers and horse thieves, a myth grew up around her under the name of Belle Starr. Whatever her involvement in crimes of various sorts with several different outlaws, a dime novelist not overly concerned with facts popularized her as "Belle Starr, the Bandit Queen, or the Female Jesse James." On her way home from a friend's house early in 1889 she was killed by two shotgun blasts. Her murderer, mostly likely someone from among her friends or family, was never found. She was forty-one.

General Joseph Orville Shelby, leader of the "Iron Brigade" with whom Will Webb and two of his Webb clan cousins rode throughout the war, refused to surrender when the war ended at Appomattox. He led a company of some one hundred and fifty men and officers from two brigades down to Mexico where he had visions of creating a colony. That misadventure ended when the Mexican Emperor, Maximilian, refused Shelby's offer of his military resources. Having never officially surrendered to the Union it was ironic for Shelby, having returned to Missouri, to be appointed by President Grover Cleveland in 1893 as United States Marshall of Western Missouri.

Granville Webb, Will's Negro step-brother began his emancipation as a farmer near Neosho and in his later years worked for a Carthage bank. Another former slave from southwest Missouri became one of America's great Negro leaders. During the war, among the many Negroes stolen from slave holding Missouri families, was an infant boy and his mother. The boy was later returned to his former owners, who lived not far south of the original Webb land. The fate of his mother was never known. His deep desire for improvement and education carried him through college, advanced studies, and a long and illustrious career as an educator and experimental botanist. His name, George Washington Carver, will forever be associated with the peanut.

The last time we see Will Webb, the protagonist of our story, he and his youngest son Jim are seated side by side in the family's buggy pulled by a black mare named Shelby. It is late April, 1917. Earlier that month on April 6, President Woodrow Wilson had signed a joint resolution of Congress declaring a state of war with Germany. Jim had convinced his father that he wanted to talk to the local recruiter who was signing up men for the U.S. Cavalry. He wanted to walk the mile to the downtown Webb City office, but to his dismay his father insisted that they take the buggy together. It was embarrassing enough to be taken in by his father but, much as he feared, on the way east up Fourth Street they passed some young women from the neighborhood. Jim knew the girls were snickering as the buggy rolled by. Try as they might, the family had not been able to convince Will to buy what he insisted on calling a "horseless carriage." There were rumors of a nickname around town, "Ole horse and buggy Will."

In truth Will was fundamentally a man of horses and had been so from his childhood through his teenage years in the war and his life as a blacksmith. In the booming mining years keeping horses properly shod and buggies and wagons repaired was still an important part of his black-smith business.

The Webb buggy rolled along at a reasonable pace, painfully slow for Jim, on up Fourth Street to the top of the hill where they turned left down Main Street following the grade down north to the heart of town. Jim was pleased not to see anyone else his age on either side of the street but he knew trouble was brewing when he saw the 1915 Model T touring car coming south up the hill. Just as the brass radiator Ford reached them, picking up speed for the hill, there was a loud backfire and a puff of black smoke. Shelby reared up. Will struggled to rein her in and freeing one hand shook a fist at the passing car. Chugging on uphill the driver was not aware that he had been cursed. "Damn infernal contraption."

Will had lost touch with his friends back in Lockhart, Texas, so he didn't know that Emil Seeliger, his eccentric blacksmith friend, had actually built his buggy with a "horse" in the box behind the driver's seat. For one hundred twenty-five dollars, including sixty dollars for the tubeless tires, he had fulfilled his dream in 1904, reaching the breath-taking speed of fifteen miles per hour on his first drive.

Jim, always a brassy and outspoken young man, couldn't restrain himself. "We Webbs are the laughin' stock of town, Father!" He was almost shouting, "Everybody in town laughs behind your back!" The old man offered no rebuttal. He knew what his true friends thought of him. For the rest, he didn't care a whit about their opinions. Age and experience had insulated him well. He had proven himself again and again in a long life full of danger and grief. It gave him, at more than three score and ten, license to live as he pleased with no apologies to anyone. Many of his peers and most young people, including his nine children, could not have imagined the challenges he had surmounted, but like many veterans he seldom spoke of the horrors of war.

Giving the reins a little snap, father and son rolled on down the hill to the recruiting office. Jim realized he had let his temper get out of control again, but couldn't think of what to say by way of apology. In fact his father wasn't expecting one.

The recruiter went through his routine, painting his picture of the war in Europe from a colorful palette of patriotism and inevitable victory. Judging that Jim must be as much an enthusiast for horses as his father obviously was, he pointed out the back window to a holding pen where a handsome stallion of at least fifteen hands stood. Thinking, as it already had done with a dozen other young men, that the promise of a fine horse would clinch the deal he said, "When you sign up son, you'll have a fine horse like that. His name's "Midnight.""

There was a long pause as the cavalry horse's name hung between the three men, none of them sure what should be said next. Jim remembered the many times through his youth that he and his four brothers had gathered at the fireplace before bedtime and begged their father to tell them again the one war tale he was willing to share. It was about how, not yet seventeen, retreating from the Battle of Springfield with the Yankees in hot pursuit, Circus, his great black stallion (the sire of generations of Webb horses including Shelby) charged up an impossibly steep hill, carrying him out of the range of Yankee fire. He could hear his father saying as he always did, "Boys, that horse Circus saved my life!"

Jim looked first at his father, smiled, then turned to the recruiting Sergeant and said, "Thank you Sir, but if I do decide to join up any horse I ride will have to be named "Circus.""

Heading home on their way back south up Main Street, just as they crossed the intersection of Broadway and Main, Shelby lifted her tail and dropped four steaming nuggets, bull's eye, at the very spot where the center line of Broadway going west crossed the center line of Main Street. She had pungently punctuated a spot where the twentieth century crossed the nineteenth century, where the Age of Will Webb (a thoroughly nineteenth century man) was crossed by a new century, where Broadway would soon become the famous Route 66, the main artery of a booming nation expanding westward from Chicago to L.A.

ACKNOWLEDGMENTS

This book has had many friends. At the head of the list is Daniel McCarron, Harvard University colleague and friend of many years. Without his encouragement and advice through the years of its gestation and his expertise in book design and print production, *Soldier's Heart* might never have seen the light of day. Another Harvard colleague and long-time friend, the late Mary Smith, was unwavering in her cheery and informed support. As a Harvard research librarian she helped me discover key facts that lie at the heart of the story. Gilbert Mudge, Jr., M.D., his colleagues at the Brigham and other practitioners repeatedly enlivened me for creative work. Paul Indelicato worked his swift magic to prepare the text for printing.

I am indebted to a number of members of the two families that appear in my tale—my maternal line, the Webbs, and my paternal line, the Rusks. They generously shared historical records, photographs, and oral tradition, and pursued important lines of research.

One the Webb side are: the late Colleen Belk whose historical research on Jasper County and the Webb line was an important resource: Sharon McChesney and her husband Wayne; the late Nita Webb; two of my great uncles, George and Earl Webb, and my late Aunt, Ruth (Webb) Harding. Closer to me with oral tradition and family records were my grandfather, William Fantley Webb, my grandmother, Julia Webb, and my mother, Martha Jane (Webb) Rusk. Related to my great grandmother, Alice (Ball) Webb, are Jeanie (Ball) Crocker and her husband Jim. They came to the process late but with great interest.

On the Rusk side are family members I knew growing up and others whom I discovered online. Closest to me was my father, Ralph Gordon Rusk, who had an encyclopedic knowledge of both the Rusk and Webb family lines. The late Lyndell Rusk spent a lifetime researching the Rusk family line and constantly surprised me with valuable pieces of information and photographs. John Sandy, the oldest in my group of Rusk collaborators, shared a wealth of information including choice pieces of Civil War era oral tradition, land and court records, and photographs. Herbert Spangler lent a hand not only with similar Rusk information but also discovered some vital information relating to the Webbs during their post-bellum exile in Texas. Included also among the Rusk related contributors are: Terry VanDyke, John LaMont, Donna Stapp, Karen Oheim, Phyllis Jo Close, Hiram Rusk, Jr. and Doris Carter Wardlow. Lewann Sowersby, an authority on genealogy and local history, whom I like to think of as an "honorary Rusk," engaged the project with great enthusiasm. She unearthed choice pieces of information about both family lines and helped me fill out my grasp of the details of nineteenth century southwest Missouri history. Equally important, she led me to obscure cemeteries where nineteenth century Webbs, Rusks and other relatives are buried. Gravestone information from the period was the key to developing a credible chronology that has served as the backbone of my narrative.

I am also indebted to a number of other persons who helped in various ways: my brother-in-law Dudley Childress and his wife Nancy, Steve Weldon, Michele Hansford, John Livingston, Jean and Bob Atkinson, Jacqueline Roberts, Carol Bohl, Bob Foos, Jeanne Newby, and Allen Merriam. Art Dodger, university colleague, novelist and friend of many years, encouraged my novelistic aspirations. Bob Chancellor provided information about Civil War re-enactment events and introduced me to the editors of Missouri magazines. He and his wife, Linda proofread the manuscript. They and Ann Storm, another high school classmate, shared the hospitality of their Missouri homes during a series of promotional events. Lastly but most importantly, words are inadequate to express my appreciation for the encouragement and patient support I have received from my wife Marianne, my three children, Michelle, Ian and Kristin and their spouses.